MS. MANWHORE

KATY EVANS

Playlist

"Firestone," by Kygo

"Want to Want Me," by Jason Derulo

"Nothing Really Matters," by Mr. Probz

"Gold Dust," by Galantis

"Paradise," by Tove Lo

"All We Need," by Odesza

"Addicted," by Saving Abel

"Kiss You Slow," by Andy Grammer

"Peace," by O.A.R.

Dear Readers,

When I finished writing *Manwhore +1,* I wasn't ready to say goodbye to Malcolm and Rachel yet. I wanted to know what happened next, I wanted to see it. For all those who wanted the same, this one is for you.

Here's to every *I do.*

BEST DAY

"*Yes yes yes yes!*"

I said yes times four, because one didn't seem like enough for my boyfriend.

This is the best day of my life.

The excitement buzzing in my veins is so off the charts I cannot sit still.

I'm having dinner with the Hottest Man on this Earth at the top of one of Chicago's premier skyscrapers. The city skyline twinkles with night lights, and a set of standing heaters blazes around us, protecting us from the cool wind. Tiny electric candles flicker down the path where my man led me out into this very terrace.

He sits across the table and neither of us is paying attention to the exquisite food the chefs brought out to us.

We can't stop touching, reaching across the table to touch and kiss each other.

My brain keeps seizing and going back to only minutes

ago, when I heard him say that he loves me . . . that he wants to marry me . . .

Oh god, *he wants to marry me.*

This man has the power to turn anything ordinary into extraordinary. A men's shirt. A green grape. A pair of necklaces. A ticket to a baseball game. An office visit. An evening. A bed.

Well, today Malcolm Saint turned my average weekly workday into the day that I became his fiancée. His one and only ever fiancée.

We are officially . . . *engaged*!

And Malcolm looks so very pleased with himself right now, his lips curled, his dark hair a little tousled by the wind, watching me through dark-as-night lashes as he leans across the table to refill my wineglass.

He won't take his eyes off me. Thoroughly and unashamedly, he watches me with happily dancing, liquid green eyes as he sets the bottle back in the silver bucket that stands near our table, and as he does, I inhale the cool breeze.

We're both still dressed for the workday, but Malcolm rocks his office attire, while I look a little bit secretarial. He discarded his sable jacket and tie a little while ago and unbuttoned the top two buttons of his shirt, and I'm in a pencil skirt and button-down top, my hair tied in a haphazard bun at my nape to keep it out of the wind.

"What are you thinking?" he asks softly as he takes my hand once again over the table and traces his thumb along the back of mine, dipping it into the hollow of my palm.

I smile at him as the silence stretches between us. The kind that is laden with words.

Words like: Are we doing this? *Yes,* we're doing this!

"I'm playing your proposal again in my head," I admit, laughing. "I'm ridiculous, I know."

He laughs softly and lifts my fingers to his lips. "Do you want me to ask again?"

A devil's twinkle appears in his eyes, and I bite my lip and nod.

His voice thickens. "Marry me, Rachel." He leans across the table, his hand on the back of my head as he pulls me in to meet his lips.

"Yes," I breathe a second before he kisses me, slow and languorous. "I love you, Malcolm," I whisper as I touch my tongue to his.

"I love you too," he husks out against my moving lips.

When we pry away from each other, my heart feels swollen in my chest with love for him. I glance at my hand and *yes* . . . there's the proof, the bright ring on my left hand, near where his thumb is still tracing the side of my palm.

I'd never seen a more brilliant diamond in my life.

The ring belonged to Malcolm's mother; it sits high in a pretty platinum band, and the rock glitters, bright and alive, even with only the moon and candles from which to refract light.

I cannot believe that this ring, this gorgeous ring, is now on my hand. Exquisitely big, sparkly, perfect. It's all I can do—just look at the ring that Saint gave me. That Saint just slipped onto the fourth finger of my left hand.

I look at it adoringly even as Saint looks at *me*.

Six feet plus of pure ruthless businessman, one with the force of a thousand storms. This eternally mysterious, phenomenal man was never in my plans. I was certainly never in *his*.

But now marriage is our future together.

Now my ultrahot fiancé is leaning back like a czar in his seat, watching me with that penetrating gaze.

Saint has been the very symbol of a player, the most wanted billionaire bachelor in Chicago, for quite some time. And I know with certainty that his guy friends and annoying female groupies are going to bust a brain vessel when they hear that we got engaged. Not to mention my friends and mother probably having a fit of panic and excitement.

"The girls are going to freak out. But I want to see their faces when I tell them." I grab my wineglass and take a sip. "Did the guys know you were going to propose?"

He takes his phone out, thumbs off a text, and sets it aside. "They do now." He grins.

And his eyes look so very liquid tonight, my legs feel rubbery at the sight.

He pushes his chair back to make room for me, and I quietly go around the table and settle down on his lap.

Saint has the perfect arms; they hold me just right. Close, but not too tight, saying *I'm here*, but not *you're trapped*. They kind of coax me to lean on him—coax me, not demand me. He is confident and this is how he attains what he wants, always with patience and persistence. He likes earning what he has.

He holds my head in one hand and thumbs my lips a little bit, as if preparing them for his kiss. "I'm going to kiss you. Everywhere. All night." He brushes a ghost kiss across the corner of my mouth, and I'm not only ready for another kiss, I'm *eager* for another kiss. I'm *dying* for a kiss that won't end until morning.

Anticipation buzzes in my veins as I melt into his hard, warm chest and feel his lips press softly into the other corner of my mouth. I sigh contentedly, and then Saint lifts my hand and kisses my knuckles and inspects the ring, getting a small frown as he studies it. "We need to get this resized."

"I don't want to take it off just yet." I cover it   possessively, then shoot him a sly smile. "I'll roll Scotch tape around one side to make it plumper and keep it in place."

"Classy," he says drolly, and as we start to laugh, both his hands curl around my skull and he sweeps down to tease his smiling lips against mine.

I tip my face up to his, and my smile fades at the sight of Saint's smoldering green gaze. I wrap my arms around his neck, hungry for him, so desperately in love with him, breathing, "Kiss me, Sin. Kiss me like we just got engaged."

He carries me down to his place. He's holding me so tight I can't breathe, but I don't want to breathe.

We undress and pet heavily for half an hour in bed, our mouths latched and savoring each other's taste, each other's warmth, each other's mouths. My mouth is red and swollen from his kisses, and my skin feels hot and tingly under his fingertips.

God. I feel like Venus. Beautiful, weak, strong, everything, as he tenderly tells me how good I taste, smell, feel.

"I really love you." Four words spoken in quiet amazement—husky and deep and just a whisper in my ear.

"I do too."

Warm fingers stroke along my curves as I rub my hands up the wall of his chest and look at his eyes in the dark.

The sheets beneath me feel so soft and like nothing compared to the hard substance of his body above mine. Strong, firm lips take me again, a perfect fit. We kiss for a long minute, stopping to nibble only so we can catch our breath.

His breath is hot on my face as he looks at me closely, in the dark. "I loved hearing that 'yes' come out of your mouth."

I smile up at him. "Mmm. *Yes*," I repeat, all sultry and wanton.

He smiles a little, and he looks so boyish and carefree. But then he grows serious again. Hungry again.

He sits up in one fluid move, pulls me on top, and fastens his mouth to my lips, never taking them off me as he drags them down my neck to suck on one of my breast tips.

The suction causes my nerves to start tingling and the blood to start boiling inside me. We sit in bed like this, my legs wrapped around his hips, his thighs beneath me, his mouth and hands devouring me. This man devouring me.

I rock my hips, slowly pleading for him to fill me. He comes back to my mouth and kisses me passionately, deliciously, deep enough to make my toes curl. My nipple beads under the brush of his thumb.

Before I realize what I'm doing, my nails are digging into his hair and I hear the low, soft pleas I make, begging, *Saint, please, I'm aching for you . . .*

The words end up a sigh that he covers with his mouth again. Our bodies shift closer, my smaller one molding to his hard, unyielding planes.

"Rachel, you're drenched for me."

A breathy gasp escapes me when he teases my entry with his erection. He rolls me onto my back and folds my legs, curling them around his shoulders, opening me. Every inch that he advances is bliss compounding on more bliss. The sharp, clean smell of his soap envelops me, weakens me. My senses overload on Malcolm Saint.

His mouth opens on mine with the same thorough deliberation he opens me with his hardness. His weight presses me down on the bed as he drives all the way inside. I groan. Saint rocks his hips to set a rhythm, his hottest parts taking over my softest ones. I pull his face closer to me and drop kisses on his thick neck, up to his jaw, as he gnashes his teeth while he enters me, over and over, harder and deeper.

My folded legs tighten against his shoulders. "Oh. More," I beg, surprised by my own breathlessness.

He gives me more, giving and taking with each thrust.

He waits for me to get to the pinnacle. Quickly, I reach it. I hear myself purl out his name. I whisper *I love you* as he intensifies his thrusts and jets off powerfully inside me.

When I fall limp, he uncurls my legs from his shoulders, lies on his back, and runs a hand down my back as I spoon at his side. I sigh in relaxation. Is love like this? Where you keep falling and falling, every day that you look into his eyes?

I hear him inhale. He's relaxed and satisfied as he tucks my face into his neck and rests his chin atop my head and strokes a hand down my hair.

What will it be like to marry him?

As if he's thinking the same thing, he looks at the ring on my hand and kisses my knuckles, wiping my sweaty hair from my face.

"Should we spend the night at my place?" I ask. "That way I can tell my friends, call my mom, and you can leave to your early breakfast."

"Sounds like a plan," he says, his voice still gruff with lingering lust.

He goes to the bathroom to clean up and when he comes back out, we get dressed.

An hour later, we're at my place, having the best sex—again.

"God, have we been making noise? Gina . . ." I breathe into his neck, tightening my arms around him, then I giggle in embarrassment.

He squeezes me, husking out, "I think we're good."

"*You're* good," I counter.

He gives me a heavy-lidded look before he kisses me for a long, long while, slow and lazy, his fingers spread out around the back of my head, and then he rolls me around to my stomach. He caresses my ass as he pulls me up to my knees and drives into me from behind. I make fists, moaning low. The bed squeaks as I clench the sheets, the engagement ring on my finger flashing as it catches light from the streets.

THE MORNING AFTER

"**O**OOOOPEN SESAME!" I hear my roommates yell through my door.

"I'm not Sesame and I'm sleeping," I murmur into my pillow.

"Speaking of sleep, you owe me sleep time. I heard you all fucking night, you fucking horn dogs—open the door!" Gina demands.

I hear the door crack open.

"Are you alone?" she asks. "I'm with Wynn."

"Malcolm just left," I admit sleepily, and the door swings wide open.

"OHMIGOD!" they squeal, and there's bouncing on my bed around my feet before they each drop down next to me. "FUCKING TELL US THAT HE PROPOSED!" Wynn cries.

I roll to my back, and my face hurts from smiling so much. I wonder why they're asking me this. Do they know me this well? I look down at my hand and . . . there's the diamond ring flashing. I couldn't take it off, not even to sleep. But I quickly cover it right now with my free hand.

"Rachel, we don't have all day." Wynn nudges me excitedly, and she seriously looks so stoked, she could be on Ecstasy right now.

"I was going to invite you guys to lunch to tell you about it."

"Dude, you still owe us lunch, but tell us now. The whole world knows and we're your best friends!" Gina counters.

"What? What do you mean the whole world knows?" I leap off the bed and whip out my laptop, then rush back under my warm covers.

"Go ahead and surf the Net." Gina gestures. "Dude, your mother probably already knows."

I open my laptop and start scouring the Net.

Within minutes, I glean the most prominent information.

a. His groupies are not happy.

b. The one who divulged to the world was goddamned Tahoe.

Well, ladies, it's official @malcolmsaint is off the market. From now on @RachelDibs gets both the Saint and the #sinner

And the replies to that came fast and furious, with commentary that basically read, in different forms:

FUCK THAT BITCH I GIVE IT A MONTH

WHATTTT!

Seriously there's no way Saint can get sated with just one! EVER!

I shut my laptop. "Nope," I say. "I'm too happy to let this spoil it."

"You can tell Saint to ask the dickhead Roth to remove it," Gina says.

"Saint's busy. It'll happen anyway, the speculation. Might as well happen now." I fall back on my pillow and my eyes drift shut as the sudden memory of last night hits me.

I'm marrying the man I am in love with, the one who takes me to Pluto and Saturn, makes me lose my senses, and makes me want to be the best I can be. Oh god.

I slide my hands under the sheets and grip my stomach. We're not using condoms anymore. I'm on the pill but I swear I can still feel him inside me.

"Well, are you going to tell us?" they yell, snapping at me to sit up in bed.

How can I deny them when they've got those puppy-dog, take-me-home, tell-us-everything eyes?

How can I deny myself the pleasure of telling *them*?

"Coffee first," I say, and after I get up, brush my teeth, and slip on my fuzzy socks, I find them sitting, with a steaming cup of coffee placed right where I usually sit.

"Wow, thank you." They're sitting across from me, waiting, smiling the widest smiles I've ever seen.

I take a sip of coffee just to seem cool—like this isn't the best thing that has ever happened to me aside from Sin—and then I nearly trip over the words of what to tell them first.

"So," I begin, suddenly overflowing with such incredible happiness that I can't seem to speak, so I just pull out my hand and show them Saint's ring.

"Are you telling Mom?" Gina croaks.

"I'm calling her right now to tell her I'm coming over. I want to tell her in person."

"Rachel!" Wynn screams, and they both hug me and urge me to call my mother.

I suppose that when you've been dating a guy for several months and you've never dated anyone before, your mother starts getting her hopes up. It seems a natural thing for a mother to want the best for her daughter. Steady job. Friends. Happiness. She watches you struggle, all while she is trying to help and simultaneously letting you spread your wings, but the very moment that your mother spots something that could make you actually happier than you already are—something that seems impossible—she sets her hopes on it.

"Have you ever discussed marriage?" she had asked only recently when I stopped by to see her one weekend.

"No. Mother! I'm twenty-three."

"I was certain he was going to propose on your birthday," she'd said.

"Stop dreaming. Plus, things are so perfect."

I'm a journalist, young still. With so much to learn. I read stories, write stories, and love stories, but I'm not a person in one of my stories. This is me, real, just human and amazed that I found what I did, that the man I've fallen in love with actually loves me, but my mother kept asking.

And that's not the only part of being in your first relationship.

Your friends start asking you about it too. They've noticed all the benefits, fund-raisers, movie nights, and they definitely noted the trip to Napa he took you on. They start noticing that the ratio of times he goes out to club with his friends versus the times he goes out with you starts leaning in your favor. And they seem to have a chart measuring all these things, as if that will tell them how serious it is. And it's serious. It's very serious. *You* know it most of all. That you're in seriously deep, you can't possibly go deeper. So your friends start to suspect he's just as serious about you too.

And they keep asking, curiously, if you've talked marriage, and they frown when you say, "No, don't be silly." As if they just added one plus one in their heads and your answer isn't two, so it's not the right one. Not the right answer, it can't be.

And despite my denials, maybe . . . no, not maybe . . . for sure, I kept hoping too. I kept wondering, after one of his smiles, those piercing, smoldering looks, I kept wondering: Does he sometimes wonder what it would be like to make me his wife?

I kept wondering if that was even in the plans.

I had hoped, and maybe fantasized, but I never expected him to propose.

I hear my friends asking for details and grab my phone to call my mom and tell her the news, and even as I tell them everything and dial her number, I cannot believe that this is me.

I cannot believe that this is *us*.

My manwhore and me.

At 9:18 a.m. I'm at my mother's. She didn't know. Emotions pass through her eyes when I tell her. Surprise. Happiness. Hopefulness. A little bit of natural worry. Then tears. We hug for like ten minutes.

I tell myself I might have not cried so much if she hadn't started rocking me as we hugged, as if I were still a little girl.

Once we've used up a box of Kleenex and have wiped our faces, I spend the rest of the hour telling her all about it.

She wants to know *when*!

How *exactly* he proposed!

And she especially loves the history of my engagement ring.

At 10:43 a.m. I'm heading for work, dreamingly staring at the passing buildings as I ride in the back of the Rolls, when I get a call from him.

"Mom's thrilled," I say when I pick up, smiling wide. "She says you did good. She especially commends you for your choice in brides."

"Speaking of my bride. She might want to consider working from home today."

"Why?"

"We've got a couple of campers outside."

"Press?"

"And their mothers and their pets."

There's a trace of annoyance in his voice, which I'm sure is there because he knows how much I hate the attention that he gets.

I exhale as I process the information.

"Security's taking care of it," he assures. "Lay low today."

"Okay," I agree. Then I lower my voice so that he knows I'm not discussing anyone else but us now. "Laying low but flying high today. I love you."

"Love you too."

At eleven, I'm back home to find dozens of floral arrangements. Flowers of all kinds are exploding colorfully out of all sorts of vases. Clear and colored, tall and short. Every arrangement has a card addressed to me in some way or another. Miss Rachel

Livingston; Ms. Rachel Livingston. I open the first.

Congratulations from all of us at Flowers and Bouquets, we'd love to do your wedding.

Dear Miss Livingston,
   Wishing you and your beloved Malcolm Saint much wedded bliss! Modern Floral has been catering to young couples for three decades . . .

And so on. And on. And on.

It's like I went to bed a normal girl, and woke up a princess. Engaged to a prince.

I gather all the cards, slip them into a brand-new manila folder I quickly label with the word WEDDING, then I sigh and eye them all. Green tea steaming in a mug, I settle down with my laptop and get some work done, then I google *wedding dresses* and take a peek and get a little thrill.

I want to be the most stunning bride my groom has ever seen.

White. For Sin. For sure.

ENGAGEMENTPARTY

We have a small engagement party with only our closest friends that night, over at Sin's penthouse. Wynn and Gina pull out their flashiest outfits because, to Wynn, "it's at Saint's place, right? I'll feel so lowly if I don't bring our best!" And because they look like exotic birds out of paradise, I pull out a dress, a little too sleepy to doll myself up much.

I know I am underdressed, but when I arrive and Sin looks into my pale gray eyes, outlined by sooty lashes that spike up with the mascara I used, I realize he's looking at me like there's not enough material to cover me—a whole new definition of *underdressed* to him.

He looks at me, checks me out in a quick sweep too, and sends a look to his friends that says *don't even look at her.* Of course, his jeans hang low on his waist in a way that I can't help but notice.

The girls trail me inside with wide eyes, obviously continuing to be stunned by the glamorous luxury of Saint's apartment. Natural stone floors, dark wood cabinets, pristine glass, shiny chrome, European leather furniture, and endless floor-to-ceiling windows—Sin's place surpasses anything they've seen, even on an *Architectural Digest* cover.

We settle on one of the lounges with direct access to the terrace and infinity pool. Warm coffee cup in my hands to help me stay awake, I take little sips while everyone else drinks like it's Friday—because it *is*.

"Getting kind of hooked on Rachel's articles," Tahoe tells Saint.

My head snaps up in surprise.

Saint smoothly answers, "They're my new religion." His lips quirk as our eyes connect for several seconds. "Catherine knows the moment I step into the office, I expect my coffee, and *Face* opened up to your column."

Liquid heat pools in my tummy. I can tell by his slow-spreading grin he's delighted to have surprised me.

We're all chatting amicably but in my peripherals, I steal little peeks of him. All of him. His hand curved around his coffee cup, overwhelming it, his thumb on the ear—my stomach swirling with heat when I remember what he did with it.

He's the only one drinking coffee too. *Thank you, sex marathon. I still wouldn't change you for the world.*

He was looking ahead as we talked with our friends but he seems to sense my stare, turns to look at me, his smile fading as our gazes lock again.

I love being seen like this. There's this sensation in the middle of my chest, tight and achy. The way he concentrates so fully on me, nothing else; just me, as if I'm all he sees. I know it's not true; Saint is always aware of his surroundings. But the kind of force with which he looks at me seeps into my bones.

Inside that gaze are a new intensity and awareness that tell me, without a shadow of a doubt, what he wants and expects from me. Truth and loyalty . . . and everything.

"So. Is she going to keep working?" Callan asks then.

"She'll be my wife; she can do whatever the hell she likes."

"Exactly, like not work," Callan says.

"She's too much a woman to shop all day," Gina says. "She has shit to offer the world, and her man's a big man; she needs to be a big girl too."

"Exactly. Am I supposed to drop everything simply because I'm the biggest Sinner that ever lived?" I turn to Saint.

"Only when I ask you to."

"Saint." I shove him playfully in the chest, and he grabs my hand and flattens it against him.

"I'm excited for you, Rachel," Wynn says. "You get a wedding coordinator, you get to pick the cake . . . please tell me you're going to do cute little figures on top?"

"No. Just . . . no, Wynn."

"Ohmigod, you have to. It's going to be the wedding of the century."

"The press is going to feast on it for weeks," Emmett says, nodding his blond head.

My stomach contracts.

Malcolm appeases me with a gentle squeeze on my shoulder. "I'll keep them out."

Gina heads off to the wine cellar, and minutes later, Tahoe stands and follows her. They end up meeting by the door. They start chatting and before I know it, I hear a familiar soft laugh.

The sound of Gina when she was with Paul. Gina when she was happy. Gina when she was *flirting*.

Tahoe, unaware perhaps of how rare Gina's laugh is, takes two bottles of wine from her and heads toward us, and Gina follows him with another bottle.

Gina grins at us and drops down in her seat. "If you ever need a pitiful friend who'll drink all your wine, I'm totally here for you, Saint." She lifts the bottle and says, "The box you sent over to Rachel created a new addiction."

"I'll make sure Rachel keeps you stocked," Saint says calmly.

I smile at Malcolm. I know he's nice to my friends because of me, and maybe they're growing on him. I still appreciate what he does.

"I'll be visiting Napa next month, Gina. You're invited," Tahoe says gruffly, watching her with his blue eyes looking bluer than usual. "After the wedding," he specifies.

Gina is frozen in place, visibly and uncharacteristically uncertain. "I'm not sure I can . . ."

Tahoe doesn't speak; he is clearly waiting for more.

Wynn straightens in her seat. "Dude, are you blushing?" she asks Gina, frowning.

"No!" Gina says, then she lowers her voice. "No." She glances at Tahoe and quickly looks away, and then she smirks and signals at me. "I leave that to Rachel."

When she speaks, I feel Saint's gaze slowly trekking across my face, greedily drinking up my quickly warming cheeks.

It's like a touch of summer sunlight, to have his eyes on me. The moment they touch me, I warm up all over.

After opening and emptying all three bottles of wine, our friends leave.

I take some of the glasses to the kitchen and then come back to find Malcolm booting up his laptop and tossing his Bluetooth headpiece nearby.

I sit down next to him again. "I don't want a big wedding. All that talk about wedding preparations . . . I just want you."

"I want my wife to have a big wedding."

"Let's go to city hall and just do it."

He kisses my lips. "I'll think about it."

"Make me your wife now."

"You're already mine. This says you're mine." He taps my necklaces. "You'll wear a ring to match. Right next to this one." He touches my engagement ring.

"Why are you determined I have a big wedding?"

"Because you're only getting married once."

"Once to *you*," I tease.

He smiles. "If I set the bar high, no one will even attempt to compete. Once to me is once."

I smile. "Okay, I'll meet a wedding coordinator. I'm getting a white dress. And the hottest groom there will ever be. Marrying *me. Once.*"

"That's what I said."

I glance at an invitation, one of the dozens that arrive per week. This time it says *Mr. Malcolm Saint and Miss Rachel Livingston.*

"What do you think it will say in a few months?"

He looks at it. "It'll say Mr. and *Mrs.* Malcolm Saint."

"Nah, it'll say Malcolm Saint and his lusty, luscious little wife who he can't get out of bed," I tease.

He laughs, then raises one dark eyebrow. "It'll say Mr. and Mrs. Malcolm Saint. And that's final."

"What about Livingston?"

"Enjoy it while it lasts."

"Sin!"

"Sinner," he absently shoots back as he reads the invitation, then shoves it back into the envelope.

"We're not in agreement yet."

"Yes we are."

"No we aren't."

"I'll get it on the prenup, little one."

I groan. Seriously. Prenups. Though I know a man like Malcolm absolutely could not marry without one. "I understand we need one," I say.

"Don't worry," he answers softly. "My lawyers insist we do this. But I'll look out for you."

"And I'll sign it then. I'll sign it because I love you and trust you and because I want to marry you."

"So do I."

"So will you indulge me? Your wife? And let me keep Livingston . . ."

"I'll indulge you in other ways. You, indulge me," he says huskily, "and take my name."

Take his name.

Because I love him.

Because when I look into his eyes, nothing else exists but him.

Because even when I don't look into his eyes, nothing else exists but him.

"I'll think about it," I say, throwing his words back at him with a smile. "And you think about the wedding."

I go slip into my jeans and a sweater, then I grab my bag.

"Where do you think you're going at this hour?"

"I have a campout with End the Violence. Remember?"

"Ah, fuck."

"You don't need to come. This is *my* passion, yours is work."

"I have a conference call: China."

"I know you do." I approach him and boost myself up with his shoulders. "Go nail it to the wall." I peck his lips and pat his flat chest. "I'll see you tomorrow."

"Rachel," he says warningly, eyebrows drawn low, "wait for Otis to pull the car around."

PEACE . . . AND WILDFIRE

I arrive at the park like never before: wholly unprepared. I forgot my chips, my music, my books. All I brought is a sleeping bag and it's hardly enough to cover me. Scanning the park, I see everybody's either quietly reading or listening to music. Some are huddled in their sleeping bags, talking.

Rather than look for someone I know, I crave to be alone, so I look for the smoothest patch of ground to lie on, and when I can't find a good one, I head toward the base of a big tree.

I take off my shoes because my feet ache and I mourn for my fuzzy socks as I tuck my feet into my sleeping bag. It's already fall. The air is quite cool tonight and thank god for my cardi.

Propping my shoulders against the tree, I tilt my head back and stare up at the leaves and the very few stars you can see in Chicago. I squeeze my eyes shut in happiness and inhale. Being here centers me. It makes me wonder about things, the coincidences in this universe, our roles in the grand scheme of things, and it reminds me that this world is full of so many people, each of our actions creating a butterfly effect in others' lives.

I think of all the stories I am going to tell now, in my platform. I want him to be proud of me. I want to be proud of myself. My dad to be proud of me. My mom to be proud of me.

And I want to be the kind of wife my husband deserves.

I hear the crunch of leaves and twigs nearby.

A tall shadow walks in the darkness toward me, and then I see the figure's incredible eyes gleam in the dark and a sliver of moonlight falls on his tan, chiseled face. I close my eyes, disbelieving, and open them in shock. And he's still walking forward with that achingly familiar walk. *Sin.*

"I'm not a dream, Rachel," he chides with a little chuckle. And his voice sounds like those leaves he just crunched, a little dry and earthy. It warms me better than my cardi. Oh god.

Butterflies.

"No tent to protect me from the elements?" I quietly tease him.

His devil's smile appears. "Just me."

"What happened to the conference call?"

"I seem to have developed a new ability that's called rescheduling."

He spreads a jacket, black as midnight, down on the ground right next to me, and signals for me to sit.

Seeing him after these intense past twenty-four hours is making me ache more powerfully than ever before. "You know, I like touching the earth." I slip my fingers into the dirt a little and then lift them and dust them off. "It grounds me."

When he only looks at me in the shadows and settles down next to his jacket, making me nervous to know what he's thinking about that makes him so pensive and quiet, I feel flutters all over me. AAARGH. We were just in bed together last night.

In fact we've been in bed every night together for more than four months.

My eyes widen when he reaches out and picks me up from the ground and straight to his lap. Every bit of him is surrounding me, enveloping me, maddening me. Malcolm turns his head and narrows his eyes when he notices, like me, that some people are whispering and pointing at us.

Self-conscious, I drop my face and his lips press warmly into my ear. "I'm going to cry when I walk up the altar."

"I'll hold you."

"I'll be alone walking up there with no dad."

"Your mom can walk you to me. And then I've got you. For the rest of your life or mine."

It strikes me that he, too, will be alone waiting for me up there. No father, no mother, just his best man and groomsmen. Saint will be the only man in my life, and I'll be the only living family that he loves.

"Did you like being an only child?"

"No."

I peer into his face. "So you'd be fine with us having two? When we're ready?"

He chucks my chin and chides me: "Where's your sense of adventure, Rachel? I was thinking more along the lines of four."

"I'm going to kill you." My eyes flare wide. "Four Saints running around the penthouse?"

"I can get a double penthouse. And nannies for each."

"I'd be fat for almost four years. Of my life!"

His eyes grow lusty as he spreads his hand widely, encompassing my flat stomach. "You'd be pregnant. With my children."

I blush. "So you want a Kyle, a Logan, and a Preston . . ."

"I want a mini-Rachel." He squeezes my tummy and looks pleadingly at me.

"Noooo. You can't have her. It's a boy first . . . my precious little Saint. See, why should we wait to get married? The sooner we get married, the more we can enjoy each other before the babies come."

"We need to wait."

"So I can sign your prenup contract?"

"That one. And the one making you my wife." He loves my greediness. I can tell he loves that I'm eager to have him. "Do you realize this is something I never thought I'd want? I can't think of anything else but making you my wife. My priority is merging your life with mine."

He looks greedy and anticipatory and strong and tender.

My walls have crumbled before him and I don't ever want them back up. My lids are heavy, but so are his. We're both tired after our sex marathon last night.

But I still want him, every second more and more.

Barely surviving the dull throb between my legs and in my heart, I lift my head and kiss his jaw and settle back down at his side, close for warmth.

"Look at me. I was just sitting on the ground . . . with bare feet. I'm a simple girl. I like simple. And I want us to get married without the world watching us so closely."

"You chose the wrong guy."

"I've got enough complexities in my guy . . . so if we have a simple wedding then we can get to the good stuff. Like a honeymoon."

"You would deny me the pleasure of giving you a big wedding?"

"I wouldn't deny you anything, much less myself."

I close my eyes, relaxing against him. Saint works so hard and leads such a fast-paced life, I treasure my calm moments with him.

"But I do want you to be my wife as soon as possible," he tells me. "And I do want to protect you from the media frenzy."

My eyes fly open. "You do?"

"You're my passion, Rachel. More than work. We'll do what makes you happy."

"What about you?"

"Either one we go for, I get what I want."

He pulls me back against him. We fall silent and just stay there, leaning against the tree trunk.

PEACE, a sign posted by a fellow camper, stares back at me. I'm doing one of the things I most love, with the guy of my dreams. My body starts relaxing into its arousal and into him. My body's on fire and my soul is serene. Peace is what I find in his arms.

Peace and wildfire.

MOMENTUM

We've settled on a small wedding with our fifty closest friends. Malcolm is making plans to fly everyone to a little island in the Caribbean exactly five weeks from now. Nobody knows but our small circle, and we plan to keep it that way. That Sunday when we finally have all our plans in motion, Saint shoots Tahoe a call about keeping a lid on it. Tahoe has been *warned*.

On Monday, we meet with the lawyers.

On Tuesday, the prenups have been drafted and signed. Saint has given me more than I even wanted—but he was insistent. He wants me to feel safe. His lawyers weren't that pleased with the terms he offered me—I could tell by their slightly pinched eyebrows—but Malcolm only had eyes for me, and he wore a perfect, satisfied smile as I signed it.

Wednesday at noon, Saint takes a lunch break to go with me and meet with Chicago's most famous wedding coordinator. He does business on his phone while I get to pick out Tiffany cake, flowers, and invitations. By the time we're done and we're heading back to M4, it seems all I need to get married is a wedding dress. And that afternoon, while hunting for dresses with Mother, Gina, and Wynn, I discover that couture wedding dresses are difficult to find on such short notice.

I still don't have a dress by Thursday afternoon when Malcolm steals me away from work. He blindfolds me . . .

. . . and the suspense is killing me.

We step off an elevator that seemed to go up forever. Then I hear the click of my heels on what sounds like a marble floor. The air smells of fresh wind and concrete. Malcolm's hand, strongly gripping mine, leads me along the darkness. Thanks to this blindfold, that's all I can see: blackness. His thumb rubs against my knuckles as he holds my hand and mumbles commands. "Careful," "hold on to my hand," "watch the boxes."

There are bubbles of excitement in my stomach as I follow him.

Where are we?

I know he's being careful to go slow, since usually one of his steps equals three of mine in heels. But he's winding through the area slowly, and then we stop, and a wall of heat is now pressing against my back. My awareness of him heightens, and a surge of anticipation floods me as I wait for him to remove the blindfold. He pushes my hair to the side and presses a hot kiss to the back of my neck before reaching up to untie the velvet covering.

"What do you think?" he whispers into my ear.

God. I still shudder when he talks to me.

I shudder when he looks at me.

Stands close to me.

Exhaling, I finally open my eyes to see sky. Pure sky, the bluest of blue, specked with clouds. A huge window spanning the width of a wall stands in front of us, and Chicago sits below us. The room is flooded in light, and the clouds outside almost seem as if they will drift right into the room at any minute.

I'm . . . speechless.

Saint's apartment is the most luxurious thing I've ever been in.

Until now.

We're inside what would make the next list of *Architectural Digest*'s most jaw-dropping apartment penthouses in the world. Twenty-five-foot ceilings. A terrace outside with an infinity pool that seems to blend into the sky. Limestone walls, marble and limestone floors. Thick wood beams crossing strong and proud from one end of the ceiling to the next. Dark mahogany cabinets. And so many windows it's like you're part of the sky.

I'm speechless as I quickly start exploring. My heels click on the floor as I trail my hands against a modern wall in soft gray tones, as elegant as you please. The place is huge. At least six thousand square feet. I see what seems to be another elevator at the far end—separate from the set of elevators we arrived in—and when I spot the sweeping staircase, I realize that it leads to a second floor.

I whirl around and look at Malcolm, who wears a black button shirt and black slacks today. He seems to pull in his surroundings like a black hole, power and money clinging to him. He fits right into the spectacular setting as if it was made for him. I give him an awed glance. "This is amazing." A sudden thought strikes me, and my eyes flare wide. "Is this . . . ?"

"Ours."

My stomach flips in excitement. "You're not teasing me?" I

laugh in disbelief.

He walks toward me and takes my hand, kissing my forehead. "Here, I'll show you around."

I just follow, dumbstruck as I look around the massive apartment/house/villa/castle nestled in the heart of Chicago.

He stops in a huge room that has a view of our park. The park where we slept together for the first time. Not slept as in sex, but just slept. For the first time. I can see it from here. I can see . . . everything.

"This is the living area," he says, in that delicious rumbling voice of his. He spreads his hands wide, and I realize there's room for at least three or four lounging sections.

"And then," he continues, signaling to the center of the room, "a fireplace can divide our lounge areas in two. Two plasma TVs, one on each side," he says, matter-of-factly.

I step in. "What? No, no fireplace. It'll block the view of the window."

I point outside.

He frowns. "I want a fireplace though. We'll read right here. Chill out by the bar."

"Well, we can put it here." I point to the back of the room.

He assesses the area. "Fine, whatever, we'll plan that later."

I smile privately, intending to bait him a little bit.

He takes my hand and I'm led through a series of corridors into another room.

This one has a wall of mirrors on one side, cabinets, and state-of-the-art gym equipment. And it connects by a glass door to a freaking *indoor* pool.

I arch a brow.

His smile is absolutely cocky. "Indoor exercise room. For when it rains and outdoor sports are out."

"Of course."

Then I'm being pulled away again. We go up a flight of stairs that stand close to the elevator.

We reach the top and I see another room with a dividing wall in the middle, and another huge window with perhaps the best view in the world. Skyscrapers sit below us and the clouds seem to be within a hand's reach. It's like we're on top of the world.

Malcolm comes up behind me. "This is our room."

I picture the bed somewhere here. *All* I picture is a freaking bed. With a thick suede headboard—a cushion for my head when he fucks me deep. I'm immediately bombarded with images of Malcolm and me lounging in bed on a Sunday morning. Laughing about something I said, a plate of grapes on the nightstand as he feeds me some for breakfast. The sun rising through our huge window. The white bedsheets tangled at our feet. His hands traveling up my back and down my legs, while he nestles his head in my neck, his lips lazily traveling along my jaw. I get goose bumps at the thought.

"This is incredible."

Turning, I wrap my arms around his waist, tipping my head up to look at his face. "Just when I'm finding my balance, you sweep me off my feet again." I kiss his neck. And then his jaw.

He cups my face in his hands and gives me a slow, delicious kiss. I break the kiss because I start to get breathless, and I look around again. We'll have a fireplace here also, and there's a door that leads to a terrace.

"Well, what about children? All of these floors too hard for them?" I ask.

He looks down at me with the most curious look on his face, his eyes searching mine with a little heat and anticipation.

"Hand-woven rugs. Plush, thick carpets for them. We'll keep them safe. I'll take care of you all."

He takes me to see the bathroom and I spot another room adjoining it. It has that perfect wood smell because, inside, there are all sorts of aisles with white-lacquered mahogany cabinets. The ceiling has a beautiful cut-glass dome that lets in the sunlight. It looks ethereal, like a church, but Saint informs me it's just my closet.

My closet? What twisted, delicious, fabulous world is this? This man will be the death of me, I swear. And I will die happy.

Saint's closet is to the other side of the bathroom, all of his cabinets in coffee-colored wood, a dome exactly like mine   but with a modern design to match the masculine mood.

Between the closets, the bathroom has two sinks, one to each side. One huge shower with the most beautiful tile design in gray and white, a waterfall showerhead hanging from the ceiling, and at the end of the room, a marble bathtub that spreads out endlessly. It's smooth and sleek, and the sexiest bathtub I've ever seen.

"That's quite a Jacuzzi."

I lift my lashes to his, and see a smile touch his eyes.

He has been watching me *all* this time.

"Enough room for you and I to play around in."

My lungs practically collapse when he says that and I can feel my heartbeat between my legs.

He just smirks and leads me down the stairs again and toward black granite counters.

"Kitchen," he says, showing me a huge island in the middle. The work is still under way but I'm amazed by how clean and tidy everything is.

Awe-inspiring colorful Murano glasses that look alarmingly by Dale Chihuly hang from the ceiling, lit from behind. Sleek cabinets frame a set of stainless steel refrigerators. The wrappings are still on. There's a pair of Wolf stoves. And vacant spots within the cabinets seem to be waiting for even more state-of-the-art equipment.

"This looks fit for a chef . . . and I can't *cook*."

He laughs softly.

He picks me up by my hips and sets me down on the counter. He pushes my legs apart so he's nestled in between, and the smell of his cologne engulfs me in our bubble. His slight scruff scrapes the skin of my neck as he kisses along my collarbone.

"We won't be doing much cooking," he murmurs. "I see you here, in my shirt." He places a kiss on my neck. "Your hair is messy, and tangled, and you're making me deviled eggs."

"Deviled eggs for Sin?" I try to laugh but it comes out choked because he's doing some very sexy stuff right now that I can't pull my mind away from enough to think.

"Yeah, or . . . waffles, crepes, or omelets," he adds, his hands rubbing against my thighs and traveling under the silky material of my shirt to my lower back.

"And you smell like roses"—another kiss—"like that shampoo you always use." He kisses my jaw again, pushing my hair back to let his tongue rub against the slight pulse on the side of my neck.

"I'm sitting right here, looking at you in my shirt, thinking about all the things I'm going to do to you later"—another delicious kiss—"in our bed."

I moan right then. He looks up to me with smoky green eyes and kisses my lips, his hot tongue rubbing against mine. I can't breathe. I hug him to me because I want him so close I want him to become part of me. His skin feels hot under his shirt. I wrap my legs around his hips.

He laughs against my lips. "I take it you're warming up to the kitchen."

I feel like my heart is going to explode in my chest because this man is everything to me, and he is here, between my legs, telling me about our future. About me making him breakfast. About our bed. Our bathtub. About our kids.

My heart gives another squeeze. I'm panting, holding on to his shoulders.

His soft hair is tickling my jaw as he starts unbuttoning my shirt. He's going slowly. Painfully slowly. His fingers rubbing against my skin, and with every button he undoes, I become undone.

He pushes the straps of my bra down and pulls my legs tighter around him. "You drive me crazy," he whispers.

I pull his head up to kiss him, and he gives me the longest kiss of my life. I am pouring myself into this kiss, letting my lips and my tongue tell him everything he needs to know. That I crave him. That I love him. That I'm completely his to have, and cherish. I see us lounging by that fireplace he wants to put in the living room, I see us having drinks in the kitchen without friends, I see us looking out at Chicago, late at night, the lights of the buildings imitating the stars in the sky.

We're home. We. Not him, not me. We. This will be our home.

We kiss for a little while, hands wandering, mouths savoring. I could go on and on like this with him, but the elevator pings and I realize we're getting company. A handful of contractors start to shuffle inside, back from the hour-long break Saint requested they take so he could show me around. Sin buttons up my shirt and I quickly arrange my hair and hop off the counter, then I wander the apartment while the contractors consult with him.

From their conversation, I hear that he bought the whole top floor and the floor beneath it. Two-level penthouse, twenty-one-foot ceilings on the bottom one, twenty-five-foot ceilings on the top one. They're being connected through a private elevator, as well as a staircase that curves upward from the lower floor, connecting to the foyer of the penthouse.

My mother used to say that a big house was every woman's dream. That is, until you moved into it, and it became a nightmare to keep clean. I can't imagine this place ever being my nightmare.

As Saint talks to some of the contractors, I walk across the empty space. He's hired an architect to design a huge play area down below. Upstairs is for our friends, near the huge bar and terrace. The floor below has another terrace where he's making preparations for a pool that's only a couple of feet deep, for the kids; there will be a mini golf as well.

He's thought of everything. Nannies' rooms. Where our children can have parties. Where we can get together with friends. He's thought of double offices. Huge bathrooms. And an extra room where I can keep a crib and a nursery upstairs. We won't move our little Saint downstairs until there are a few more and he's a little older. Our spot of paradise in Chicago.

And I get my own closet.

I walk back to our room and admire it. Even the bathtub has a view, I see now that I admire it again. On one side I can watch the city. On the other I can watch my husband in the see-through, pristine glass shower.

Life is full of tough choices.

NOTRE DAME

Saint speaks at the University of Notre Dame on Friday. He talks about building momentum for start-up businesses during an hour-long conference in a packed auditorium flooded with the youngest, brightest minds in the country.

Notre Dame is one of the oldest universities in the country and, I've just decided, it has to be one of the most beautiful. When we drove into the campus it was like driving into another world. It consists of 1,250 acres of land, with huge old trees growing amid modern Gothic buildings—one of the largest of which is topped with a regal gold dome.

We drove up for the conference, but we stay for the rest of the day so that we can look at the stadium, the library, and some of the chapels, many of which are actually situated in the residence halls. We have lunch with the dean of the College of Business and we're heading back to the city when Sin gets a call from Tahoe. The Bluetooth picks up. I'm still dazed about the beautiful campus straight out of *Harry Potter* when Tahoe's voice flares out from the Bug's speakers.

"Saint!"

"What's up, T?"

"I've got four words for you. Bachelor Party. Monte-fucking-Carlo."

He shoots me a sidelong glance, a glint of humor lighting up his eyes. "Can't. I've got a packed schedule with the wedding coming up. Need to get everything set if I want peace during my honeymoon."

"Bachelor party. Monte-FUCKING-Carlo, Saint."

"Can't." Malcolm calmly keeps driving. "Unless you want to move it to Dubai. Got a project I'm cracking open soon."

"Fine. Dubai's our baby. When do we leave?"

"Next Friday, seven a.m. at O'Hare."

"About time I tested out that new G650 of yours. How about some bikini-clad flight attendants?"

Another sidelong glance. This one with even *more* sparks dancing in his eyes. "Got to say, T. You're on a roll here. You just went up high on Rachel's blacklist."

"Ah, well damn. Hey, Rachel," Tahoe says.

"Hi, Tahoe."

"And it's a no on the flight attendants," Saint says, reaching out to cut off the call. "No monkey business in my Gulfstream."

He cuts off without a goodbye, and I look at him.

"You men don't lose time with pleasantries, do you? No hello, no goodbye, just in and out."

He speeds up a little on a stretch of highway that's pretty clear, and chuckles low in his throat.

"Girls. Really?" I frown.

"Gambling," he counters. "And business comes first."

"Sin . . . no touching the girls. Or I swear I'm going to get a Chippendale and make out with him just to see if you like it."

His eyes twinkle. "I don't. Like it. So it's not happening."

"I'll think about it. While I spread whipped cream on   his chest and lick his nipples."

His brows shoot up now. "You'd do for a Chippendale what you don't do for me?"

"I'd do it for you next Saturday.   Oh, wait! You won't be *here*."

He laughs, then he frowns thoughtfully and keeps on driving. "I'll stock up on whipped cream."

"Okay."

"I want it all over you."

"Okay."

We're entering the outskirts of the city. I'm absolute lava in my seat, noticing Malcolm's voice has gone raspy and thick. Noticing the green shade of his eyes has darkened considerably.

"They're going to bring girls for sure."

"There are girls everywhere. You're my girl."

I look at his hands on the gearshift and the steering wheel. He's got great hands, perfect hands, and he knows how to use them like nobody's business. I don't want them on anyone else.

"And Rachel." A dark warning enters his tone, as if he's also thinking about me and the Chippendale. "My girl doesn't   get touched, or touch another man."

The possessiveness in his voice brings out a tingle between my legs. "My guy doesn't touch any other girl."

"He doesn't want to."

When we reach my building, I'm hunting for the keys to my apartment inside my bag when he pulls the door open for me. I grip the keys in my palm as I step out, and Malcolm's looking down at me with tender heat, like he wants his hands all over me too.

Like he wants to *devour* me, right here and right now,

whipped cream or no.

"Mr. Saint, Miss Rachel," Otis says to greet us as he walks over from the Rolls-Royce parked just ahead.

Saint leads me toward my apartment building and then pulls the door open for me. He holds the door open with one shoulder as he takes a pile of boxes from Otis and tells him, "I'll see you upstairs." We head into the elevator. Someone is buzzing his phone.

"Callan?" I ask.

"Probably."

I laugh good-naturedly. "You guys are incorrigible."

Incorrigible, and such boys at heart. But I love that they genuinely care for one another.

He follows me to my apartment door. Before opening my place, I whirl around and search his face. "Are you sure you're ready to share all your space with me?"

He leans his dark head down without any hesitation and takes my mouth in an all-lips, heated kiss. "I'm sure. Let's get you packed."

MOVING IN

Our new apartment will be ready in six months, so I'm moving into his place in the meantime. My mother, Wynn, and Gina are helping with the last of my boxes.

I've already transferred several boxes this morning with Otis.

Already at Sin's place are: A box with pajamas. A second box with important papers—birth certificate, passport. Some of my articles. My baby album, which he skimmed last night, start to finish—teasing me ruthlessly on my most embarrassing pictures and then kissing me to tell me how pretty I was. I've sent another box with my accessories. Photo albums, photo frames. My slowly emptied bedroom fills me with both dread and excitement of what's to come.

Now the girls and Mom are helping me tackle the rest.

"Dude, I heard you two in the shower this morning. You giggling. His voice was all low but it's still deep enough to be heard in my room. Plus the noise of all that water slapping muscles."

I lift my head from where I am organizing my cosmetics, getting ready to pack them, and my eyes widen. I remember him soaping me up, and *me* soaping *him* up—hot hands and hungry mouths and teasing touches and lathering fingers and the way he lifted me and lowered me down on him—and a hot blush creeps up my neck as I remember the rest.

"Oh god. I'm sorry, Gina. I wasn't thinking." Then, frowning a little, I lift my index finger in the air, to be clear. "But I'm not sorry about the shower sex."

Gina just smirks and continues to help shape the flat boxes into usable square ones.

"Can we make a suggestion?" Wynn asks as she finishes cutting bubble wrap into squares. "Cut the sex until the wedding."

I scowl and start opening my dresser drawers to be sure they're empty. My mother finishes taping a box closed, then heads to the next full one, peering up slightly at that. "I think that's a great idea, Rachel."

"No, Mom. Trust me. It's not."

Wynn starts to wrap all my photo frames in bubble wrap and tuck them into a box labeled FRAGILE. "Think about your wedding night. You'll only have one of those. Don't you want him to be wild for you?"

I look at them.

They don't know that Malcolm enjoys me like saints enjoy holy water and sinners enjoy sin.

We've been having sex daily, several times a day. We need it like food and water.

"You guys don't know what you're talking about."

"Imagine how much more smoldering that first night as man and wife will be," Wynn says, eyes bright with excitement.

"I definitely didn't sleep with your father the whole month before. It drove him crazy but that's why I got pregnant so fast with you."

I shoot her a wide-eyed look, then *her* eyes widen as she realizes what she said.

"Mother! TMI!"

"He would wait until the wedding night if you asked him to," Wynn advises. "Saint has been patient when it comes to you."

I shake my head, refusing to speak more of it.

Finished filling up my makeup box, I glance around to see what I need to tackle next. The room is looking sparse now, save for the big things. Which are staying. All the furniture stays here with Gina and her new roomie. Wynn is supposedly considering canceling her lease and moving in. I plan to beg her to because I don't want Gina to feel lonely, and I'm afraid that the month I'm on my honeymoon there will be loneliness here to spare. Even though Gina assures me that she's "good."

Wynn leaves the box of fragile items for my mom to tape and then walks toward my bed. "Are you taking your pillow?"

"No."

"How can you not take your own pillow?"

"I don't know. I like to lie on his chest."

"What if one day you guys are mad and there's no awesome chest?" Gina counters, opening a new flat box to make a box for the pillow.

"I hope even when we're mad I get to lie on his awesome chest. Or his awesome shoulder. Or his awesome pillows. In his awesome bed. No, no pillow."

"Oh, you! Well, this pillow's mad."

She hits me with it, and I grab it, squeeze it, and toss it back on the bed with a little pang of remorse.

It *is* my pillow. It is my room. My apartment. But if I clutter my future with too much of my past, there won't be room for the new. And the new—even though a little scary—is something I'm looking forward to.

We take a lunch break, and my mom goes to her canasta game. Wynn and Gina stay until Otis helps us load the rest of the boxes. By the time we come back up, sweaty and exhausted, I'm done, my room looks bare, and pretty, and . . . I look at it harder.

I sit on my bed. My single-Rachel bed. I look at Wynn and Gina, who are looking at me with mixed emotions from the door. Emotions like "how exciting" and "we miss single-Rachel" and everything in between.

I love single-Rachel. But she was never as happy as I am now.

"Wynn, I hope you come live here. It's such a good little room. I've got great memories here."

That evening, I'm finally at his place. Malcolm's on a phone call when I arrive, and he trails off when I walk in. I had showered and changed and I am wearing a tight tracksuit and a ponytail. He's in tan slacks and a black button shirt, and both of these clothing articles fuck his body every which way possible.

I melt first. Then I wave at him hello, walk up to kiss his jaw, and feel him give my ass a little possessive squeeze, his eyes meeting mine—hot and approving and welcoming.

I mouth: *I'm going to go and invade your male space.*

And as he murmurs something in German into the headset, he lifts his thumb and rubs it against the corner of my lips, his eyes silently saying, *It's all yours to invade.*

God.

He makes my knees go weak, this fiancé I've gotten myself.

I go start making myself some room in Saint's closet and en suite bath.

I hang all my clothes to the left side of the closet and put my sweaters, jeans, and shoes on one of the shelves next to rows and rows of identical designer items.

I'm finding space for my lipsticks and stuff in his bathroom when he stalks in, still speaking into the headset. A little cold, a little demanding. Kicking off his shoes, he yanks his shirt out of the waistband of his slacks and I can't stop looking at him.

I can never seem to screw my head on right when he's near.

Today, especially, when I think of how awful it would be to not have sex with him.

Torture.

Purgatory.

Absolute torment.

No, no, no, no abstinence.

My Sin is physical and hot for me, and I'm always a wet mess for him.

It would be hell for us. Hell.

I take off my shoes, kick them aside. At the sound of them falling he looks down, and then frowns a little as he stares at my legs, hugged by my tracksuit. He looks at my hand, my ring, smiling to himself, and his eyes slide up to meet mine.

And he looks so possessive right now.

Right now . . . that I moved in.

My stomach gives a squeeze and my hormones just won't stay under control.

Not touching him?

By *choice*?

Alas, it's only so that you can have the most perfect wedding night, Livingston, I tell myself.

And the thought of our wedding night makes me even hotter.

He unbuttons his shirt. Seeing him bare-chested causes a whirlwind in my body, unstoppable. Tanned pecs, tight brown nipples, flexing biceps, all promising to wreck me again. I want to look away, survival instinct, my body too wired, too tense, but I am thirstily drinking him up, the way his shoulders stretch as he removes his shirt, how his dark hair gleams under the lights, the small smile on his lips that reaches all the way to his eyes when he finally cuts the call and pulls off his headset, setting it aside.

"My . . . invasion was a success. As you can see. It's all yin and yang now," I say, my voice thick with lust.

Still bare-chested, he opens a drawer on the side I just overtook and peers inside. "Pink."

"Yes."

I see him check out the second drawer on the same side. Also mine. While he scans all of my neatly organized cosmetics, clips, toothbrush, and comb, I tug the hairband that has been holding my hair back and send my hair tumbling down my shoulders.

I tap the outside of a drawer on the opposite side of the sink. "This side is yours. And that side is mine." I signal to my side, with the pink stuff, and grin.

His green eyes look liquid like seas as he slowly winds an arm around me and pulls me to his chest. "You're mine."

My breath catches happily, and our eyes meet. We both look so satisfied right now, it's like we're smiling with our eyes.

And suddenly I *burn* with need.

I want those hot eyes.

I want him to look at me with those eyes on   our

honeymoon. Eyes that inflame me like they do now. That unapologetically say that they want me, and only me, for eternity. I take his hand and lead us into the bedroom, and then I let go and just stand there, visually making love to his features.

I *adore* this man.

God, I adore him so much that I can't fathom ever surviving losing him again.

He's unzipping my tracksuit jacket and my body is swiftly responding to what I know is coming next.

I want it so much my throat feels tight with raw need, but as Malcolm smiles down at me and I feel the weight of his smoldering green gaze on me, I suddenly ache to see those eyes smolder just like *this* on our wedding night.

"Malcolm . . ." I begin, curling my fingers around his hand to stop him.

And suddenly I know that I'm going to do this, that I will only have one wedding, to this man. One wedding night in our entire lives. Waiting to be with each other again would be so worth it. Because my guy, *he* deserves a perfect bride and a wedding night that he will never forget.

And I want to be that bride, I want to be the girl that he can't wait to touch, that he can't wait to be inside of.

"I was thinking about possibly . . . abstaining from sex until the wedding."

I step back a little, fighting my own hormones and need for this man.

He looks at me intently. His smile starts to disappear as he lifts one dark eyebrow. Then two. "You're not kidding."

I slowly shake my head. "Unfortunately no." I gaze into his eyes and already miss him. "This would make the wedding night so perfect. Almost like the first time. I mean it's just a week and we'll be busy anyway."

"Are you asking me? Or telling me?"

"If I ask you, you'll say no."

"So you're telling me." The eyes looking at me through those sable lashes are already brimming in frustration. They're silently demanding that I say *no*.

But I can't. I only nod.

He laughs and scrapes his hand down his face.

"Saint . . . come on."

"Do I get you one last time? Before the wedding?" His hungry tree-bark voice is back full force. "Do I?"

I walk toward the window to gather my strength, then turn. "I need to do this cold turkey or I can't do this at all."

With long, purposeful strides, he comes over and lifts me in his arms. "I strongly disagree." A warning cloud settles over his features.

"Come on. Please."

He shakes his head and sets a soft kiss on my lips. "Not for a thousand pleases."

"Four thousand?"

He sets me down on my feet, but keeps me so close to him that he leaves no room between us at all. He frowns as he looks down at me. "I get you tonight. All night."

"Malcolm. You're a shark in negotiations. You'll say another night tomorrow and so on."

"I never change the deal," he says calmly. "This is irrelevant to our wedding night."

"But it's not."

He takes my chin between his thumb and forefinger and angles my face upward, his voice uncompromising yet oddly gentle. "I get you tonight, Rachel. All night. No sleep. Nothing but you naked under my sheets."

My sex is swollen and clenched in need, my knees rubbery.

The mere thought of not having Malcolm again until the wedding is *painful.*

Saint's expression is calm, but the look in his eyes is raw and primal, possessive and determined.

He waits patiently for my answer, and as I battle inside, he ghosts the pad of his thumb across the corner of my lips, and I moan softly and tremble.

I cannot deny him one night; I cannot deny myself one night.

"Okay," I say.

One beat later, he bends to my ear and whispers my name in pure male lust—*Rachel*—his lips curving sensually as he inches back and fucks me with his eyes. Then he scoops me up and tosses me on the bed, falling on top of me.

"Saint!" I cry, laughing in protest, but he smothers my mouth with his hot one and I curl my limbs around him, needing him to breathe.

DRESS

I'm sore and fucked to within an inch of my wonderful life the next day, and I'm thinking about sex with him all through the next week as I shop for the honeymoon to . . . *somewhere.*

"Cold or warm?" I ventured on Monday.

"Warm. That's all I'm going to give you."

"East? West? North? South?"

He simply looked at me with mysterious eyes and handed me two credit cards with the name Rachel Saint. A platinum Visa and a black Amex.

I've had a bit of trouble getting used to using them.

First, because it kind of turns me on! But so is the abstinence, even if it's killing me. Saint's kisses are longer, almost as if he wants me to be in a constant state of hyperawareness until the wedding.

I've hit all the high-end department stores in search of the perfect outfits. I've forced myself to use the cards and I've noticed, a little bit annoyed, that upon the sight of the cards, the salesladies buzz around me like bees to my guy's honeyed money. I bought bikinis, cover wraps, soft, flowy dresses, tight dresses, lingerie and baby dolls and nighties.

If only it were this simple to find my wedding dress.

On Thursday, after no news from the stores or the designers they'd contacted—Vera Wang, Reem Acra, Yumi Katsura, and Monique Lhuillier—my mother summons me to her house. I take an early lunch break and head over there.

The door swings open and she spreads out her arms, and I walk into them and squeeze her. She doesn't have a lot of words, at least not in the beginning. She simply pulls my hand out, discreetly brushes the corner of her eye at the sight of my engagement ring, and ushers me inside.

"You look slimmer. You always slim down when you have too many things on your mind and forget to eat," she says as she leads me to her paint studio. "How is the move coming along? Do you need any more boxes?"

"No. I'm leaving the furniture with Gina, the bed too, for her new roommate. Just my belongings. I'm almost done."

"Is Wynn really considering moving in with her?"

"I hope so."

I nod and let her reveal the artworks she's been doing for the covers of *Face*.

"Mom, they're exquisite."

"Truly, Rachel?" she asks hopefully.

"I *love* these! Let me take pictures."

I use my phone to snap pictures of all five of them then hear my mother call me. "Rachel, come. I want to show you something."

I follow her voice into her room as she extracts something from the very back of her closet.

"A few years ago I had it vacuum packed to preserve it. It's like new. I didn't even eat *cake* in it," she says excitedly.

She hangs a long white dress on the top of the door, and I gape as I take it in. Simple and satiny, formfitting, with sleek shoulders and an elegant cleavage, a skirt that flares to a mermaid tail.

My mother insists I try on her wedding dress. "You would look so lovely in this dress."

I have a ton of mixed emotions as I look at it. Among them is a wave of nostalgia so very deep, I get a little itch in my windpipe.

This is the dress my mother walked to the altar in as my dad watched. And after only a year he would never see her, and we would never see him, again. I reach out to touch it but pull my fingers back, guarding myself against the pain it could bring. "But it's yours, I don't want . . ."

"Everything mine is yours. Please. Indulge me."

I inhale, but she looks so hopeful I can't bear *not* to indulge her.

I unhook the hanger and slip into the bathroom to undress and ease it on. I step outside without even looking at myself, without even breathing.

My mother can't conceal the look of delight and emotion on her face when I emerge from the bathroom. Then her brows pinch and she eyes it critically as she circles me and inspects me with the thoroughness of a professional tailor. "We need to tuck it in around here. And the waist and hips. Just a tad." Her eyes glisten.

"Mother . . ." I begin.

" 'Mother'? So serious? Since when do you call me Mother?" She frowns and hovers over me. "Please say yes."

"I . . ."

"It would mean so much to me! For good luck."

My eyes water. "But Dad died."

I cover my mouth, my eyes widen, and I can't believe I just blurted that out loud. I cover my face, ashamed.

"But when he was alive, we were perfectly in love. We lived the most perfect romance." She tips my face. "Rachel, I know who you're marrying. I know that you want this day to be perfect. That you want to look and feel like you deserve to be the woman walking up onto that altar. And you are.

"You're the right one because he chose you and you chose him. Rachel, no dress will dictate your future. It dictates how you feel . . . on that day. That's it. Because trust me, I know enough about him to know he couldn't care less what you wear, so long as you walk up that altar to him. I see the way he looks at you. You've been here on Sundays in sports clothes, in dresses, in jeans; he was here when we flash-painted that first cover for *Face*. You were streaked with paint, and he couldn't take his eyes off you. You could wear black or pink and that man will *still* love you."

I'm silent as I go and take off the dress.

Malcolm wants to give me a big wedding because he thinks that's what I deserve. I want to be the perfect bride because I think that's what *he* deserves. But I know for a fact that every time we talk about the wedding, our main focus, what we're looking forward to, is not the wedding itself but simply getting *married*.

When I step back into the bedroom with the dress in my hand, my mother takes it and begins to tuck it away.

"Mom, let's . . . let's alter it. Let's make it perfect for me."

Her eyes widen, then her face softens.

"Thank you, Rachel."

We hug. And just like that, I have my dress.

THE DAY BEFORE THE
BACHELOR TRIP

I step off the elevators and into the top floor at M4 and head to Catherine's desk. "Is he busy?" I ask.

"For you? Or for the rest of humanity?" She shoots me a smile and rings me in. Then she comes around her desk and walks me to the frosted glass doors.

I grab the handle, but she puts a hand on my shoulder to stop me. "Rachel."

She has my attention, but I watch a play of emotions on her face as she seems to struggle to start. "I've been with him almost ten years." She nods toward the office. "Since his mother died, and he was estranged from his father. He was the one who put me through business school. He could've had his pick of top graduates, yet he picked me. I saw him fight when there was no one to cheer him on. I saw him get better just to spite his father, to show him. I've seen him do everything he was told he couldn't do just to prove to himself he can. But I'd never seen him fall for a girl until now. I wish you both the very best.

Really."

Though I've always known Catherine has a helpless crush on Saint, she looks genuine. She looks happy for us.

"Thank you," I say and give her a quick hug, then ease through the frosted doors into his lair.

Sin winks at me in greeting. He's wearing jeans and a green sweater that brings out the forest in his eyes.

Sparks fly as our gazes latch and we smile at each other. My stomach flips. My toes curl in my pumps.

Tearing his eyes free of mine, he goes back to business as he drops back into his chair and waves his assistant over. "Catherine."

Saint makes a change to some contract stipulations, initials them, then signs his name on the last page and slides the documents over to her.

"I will FedEx these ASAP, sir. The blueprints for the extended parking lot are here."

"They're here. But not on my desk?" His brows go up, but his eyes sparkle in amusement.

When she explains the reason, he leans back and listens in that closely sophisticated, natural way that he pulls off so easily. Behind his desk, he nods and thanks her, then he prowls over to where I'm standing by the window.

He holds the back of my neck and brushes a kiss to my temple. "Hey. Didn't want to wake you this morning."

"Can I show you what my mother did for our next covers?"

I stretch out the folder to him.

He takes it in one hand and reaches out to run his knuckles down my cheek with the other.

My body crackles as the touch bolts through my veins, heating me all over.

"Impressive." He's concentrating now on the cover shots.

His head bent. So beautiful he's like from another species.

He slowly shuffles through them, scanning each of them thoroughly while I scan *him*.

Oh god.

How I love and need this one man.

"Does one scream at you?" I ask, trying to read his unreadable profile.

"I like the one with your handprint. You open with that article on End the Violence. Talk about what you want. Issue after issue, keep setting the stage, directing your readers' expectations." He scans them again. "I'd follow with this one. The world. Cementing the human interest part of the magazine."

I edge nearer and take a long, discreet whiff of him as I point to one of the shots. "And if I start with the world, *then* on the next issue, use my hand?"

He turns his head to look at my profile. His voice low—slow, like midnight-hour sex. "Works. Keep the scope wide, then zoom in." I look into his eyes and smile, buzzing like I do every time I stand close to him. He looks at me with that same wonder my mother speaks of and my stomach contracts, hot and tight. "I'm proud of you," he says.

He glances at the ring on my left hand. I just had it perfectly resized to fit my finger.

"So I was thinking I'd cook you dinner. Or attempt to, tonight." I count with my fingers. "I can make a salad, get some loaves of freshly baked French bread, some really good deli meat . . ."

"I'll tell you what." He lifts me up, carries me to the edge of his desk, and sits me down, holding me by the hips as he leans forward. "You do the salad, warm the bread, I'll make pasta."

My lips curl upward. "Nobody ever cooked me dinner but

my mama and grandmama."

His brows go up. "Will I get to meet this gentle grandmama?"

I shake my head. "She's gone."

His smile fades, replaced by concern. "I'm sorry."

He's still holding me by the hips, leaning so close that I could kiss him. "You can really cook pasta?" I ask softly.

His smile turns cocky. "Just wait and see."

"I'm impressed."

He shoots me a look that says *You haven't seen anything yet.* "Been a bachelor," he tells me.

"You've been a bachelor with *chefs*," I shoot back.

The twinkle I love so much dances in his pupils as he slowly nods. "That's right. I've learned a few tricks along the way."

"I'm all too familiar with your tricks." I laugh, thinking about his ghost kisses, his seduction, his teasing. "A perk of dating such a worldly man is getting firsthand, front-row seats, and personal with his tricks."

Silent, he simply looks at me with that wondrous smile. Then, again, his knuckles run down my cheek. "The perks of marrying him," he whispers hotly down at me, "will be even greater."

I'm breathless, flushed and warm under his looks when I finally breathe out, "You have yourself a date."

It was heaven, even though I was in abstinence *hell.*

I tried not to notice. Tried to be strong. But I wasn't the least bit immune to watching Saint cook for me. Guys in kitchens are hot. And Saint was setting the kitchen on fire just by being there, tall and easy, confident and quiet. His hair in one eye, his hands chopping easily, a ton of spices for the pasta. Rolled shirt sleeves to reveal his thick forearms.

We had an amazing time. We laughed. Had dinner on the terrace next to the outside fireplace. Drank wine. Ate. Even toasted to great teamwork on our first kitchen efforts because the food turned out surprisingly well.

At night I slipped into one of his white men's shirts, and we curled up in bed. He kissed me, gently caressed me over his shirt, and I returned the thorough, delicious attentions of his mouth with the abandon of a teenager. I bit the hard skin between his neck and shoulder, then rubbed his bare chest and tried not to think about the way his lounge pants were straining. When we were too worked up to continue, we lay in silence and I was held in those arms. I laid my head on his chest and he set his chin on top of my head, and we slept.

In the morning he woke me up to say goodbye. Freshly showered, he pressed a ghost kiss to the fringes of my mouth. My guy. My bachelor. Going off with his buddies to work and play.

"Have fun," I whispered, giving him a ghost kiss back.

"I will." He looked down at me for a long moment, his eyes going hot after my ghost kiss.

"I'll miss you."

"Take care of my girl for me."

"Take care of my guy."

And he left. He texted me before taking off:

Next time it's you, and me, and whipped cream.

And I died.

Now it's night in Dubai, and day in Chicago. A dreary Malcolm-less Saturday in Chicago. Saint's bachelor party is well under way while I am in my apartment with Wynn and Gina, drinking wine and stalking social media for a whiff of what his friends had planned for him.

@malcolmsaint CONGRATULATIONS!

I hope @malcolmsaint keeps my number for when they're done

@RachelDibs YOU ARE SUCH A BITCH I HOPE HE DUMPS YOU

I think men with wedding bands are HOT call me anytime @ malcolmsaint

Now that @malcolmsaint is off the market maybe I stand a chance in hell with the club chicks

I go back to read his last message for the thousandth time.

"You are obsessed," Gina leans over and says smartly. "No more words are magically appearing, you know."

Next time it's you, and me, and whipped cream.

"I know," I admit.

"Well, stop staring at it!" She laughs.

I smile. "It's a joke." Message reread, I close my eyes.

"Saint is Rachel's reward for torturous years of being single," Wynn says happily.

"There's nothing from Dubai," Gina states. "But people are hanging on to news of the wedding."

Wynn and Gina watch me closely.

"You're jealous that he's in Dubai?" Wynn asks.

I laugh and dismiss the observation and I pour from one of the wine bottles that Saint gave me once—my favorite. I sip and look at the fourth finger of my left hand. My newly resized ring.

"I think it's healthy for a relationship if everyone gets time to hang out with their friends."

I pour a little more wine.

"And every man has a bachelor party. I'm happy he's saying goodbye to his old ways."

My bachelorette party consists of Valentine, Sandy, Wynn, and Gina, and the wine box Saint had sent after our first wine tasting. I'm drunk by the time it starts and I doze throughout most of it.

I have a nightmare . . .

"Saint!" the girls squeal as he watches two groupies and me swim in the water from the deck of *The Toy*. "Saint, Saint, please, Malcolm Saint!"

I hold my breath when his hands go to flick open his shirt buttons. "All right, girls."

My eyes widen as he shrugs off his shirt. The blood courses through my veins, suddenly swollen by the fast pounding of my heartbeat. Large, long-fingered, tanned hands tug on the drawstrings of his swim trunks, and my eyes blur when he actually strips them off and for the three seconds he stands on the edge, I see him all. I see everything. I see that he is hard. That he is perfection—ripped, cut, narrow-hipped, broad-chested; long and muscular legs, thick and lean arms. I'm boiling in the water and I can't take it. I dip my head under, squeezing my eyes shut until I hear the water crashing as he dives in.

When I come up, he surfaces with a laugh and smooths his hair back.

"Oh god!" The girls start swimming over, and I can hear the harsh, uneven sounds of their breathing as they try reaching out to him in soft, husky pleas. "Saint, you're so hot," one whispers. "Can we stay over? Sleep over tonight, Saint?"

"Not tonight," he says, ducking into the water before they reach him. He leaves them both pouting behind him and pops up behind me and pokes my back. "Hey," he says.

I notice the girls hop onto the yacht and each of them slips into one of his white shirts.

A pulsing knot forms in my stomach as I turn and stare into his green eyes and we just float there, staring, and there seems nothing else but dark water, the sky above, and him, the darkest thing that's ever had such a pull to me. "Hey," I say.

"Come here," he whispers.

I start awake.

It's 5 a.m. in Chicago—which would make it 3 p.m. in Dubai—and the girls are still partying and wake me.

"Rachel, pick up your phone," Gina says.

She's got her iPhone pressed to her ear as I stir and groggily search for mine. She lowers hers for a moment and tells me, "They're flying. Your man's as good as married. He seemed to leave his dick home. Hang on." She places it on speaker and I hear Tahoe's Texan drawl.

"Congrats, Rachel. You're still his number-one girl. There were redheads, brunettes, double Ds. Carmichael and I got them all."

Gina takes him off speaker, and I grin like a dope because I'm still the apple of my Sin's eye.

"He wants to talk to you."

"Tahoe?"

"Saint!"

Leaping forward, I take the phone, my voice groggy and slurring with sleep. "Hello, *bachelor.*"

His voice is husky with drink and no sleep. "Hello, bride."

The words feather all over my body. There's something so warm and enchanting in the way he says "bride."

Hmm, just a tad possessive too?

"I'm flying this bird straight home. Nonstop. Full speed," he says quietly.

I clench the phone tighter as my body grips in complete anticipation. "Okay. Did you have fun?"

"Lots," he says. But he sounds weary. Weary of traveling maybe?

"Did you miss me?"

"Lots more. I called you, but no answer."

Belatedly, I realize that Wynn, Gina, Valentine, and Sandy are watching me with curious looks, so I move to the window and lower my voice. "I slept through my party."

"No whipped cream, baby?" His voice drops an octave, and I think I detect a silken thread of warning in his voice.

"No."

"Good." His voice, though quiet, has an ominous quality. "I'll keep my record clean of murder for now."

I make my tone match his. "I guess I'll let the brunettes, redheads, and double Ds live for now."

He chuckles, a laugh that's long and soft, so close that I remember how warm his breath feels when he laughs in my ear. "Mrs. Saint," he begins, unapologetically delighted, "you're an angel."

"And you, Mr. Saint, are a devil."

"In fifteen hours your devil's home."

When I hang up, everything in me has gone *butter.* My thighs *butter,* my heart *butter,* with the added bonus of *butter*flies in my tummy too.

HOME

Since it's a fifteen-hour flight, I get to hang around with the girls, a little hungover for the day, then by early afternoon I head to the penthouse to shower and change.

By 7 p.m. I am waiting for him in his apartment, wandering around a little bit and fixing my things. I don't want my Rachel Invasion to wear on him too soon, and I was a little less careful when I had a bedroom all to myself.

Exhaustion wears me down. But if my head touches our bed, I'll be asleep. I curl in the seating area in the living room, with a perfect view of the elevators to one side and Chicago to the other, and stare out the window, watching the flickering city lights as I doze off.

I hear the elevator ting and I perk up as adrenaline shoots me to my feet.

It's like electricity ignites in the room the moment Malcolm steps into the penthouse.

I see him, he sees me. The air heats and crackles like a   live thing, leaping in arcs from him to me, from me to him. His gaze latches on to mine and my heart dances as I stare at him with homesickness and longing and happiness times a million.

The air of confidence around him radiates like a power line, lures me like a flame in the dark.

He drops his luggage. "Wow, look at you."

There's a jolt of excitement in me when I recognize the admiration in his voice. I'm wearing one of his white button-down shirts for sleep but it never ceases to amaze him. I rasp, "Look at *you*."

"How are you, Rachel?"

A wave of intense feelings overtakes me as I nod over his concern. "How are you?"

"Good." The prolonged anticipation of the moment before he walks forward to take me in his arms is almost unbearable. We exchange a huge hug. A hug that is tight and warm and goes on for a minute, telling me that he missed me. His nearness kindles me to a burn as I savor the strength and warmth of his embrace. He smells of the leather of his brand-new airplane. And wood. And soap. And Saint. *Oh god, Saint.*

"Glad to be home."

"Really?"

The truth in his eyes is nearly heartrending. "Really." He smiles down at me as he spreads a hand on my face to brush my hair back, then he opens his other hand on the small of my back and smashes me to his chest to greedily fit his lips to mine. I'm all too willing. Ready. Soft. And warm.

"Oh god, I missed you, Malcolm," I breathe, sliding my hands into his hair.

"I missed you too." He sucks on my lower lip, then he sweeps into my mouth one more time, groaning, "Next time I hit Dubai, you're coming with me." He reaches into the back pocket of his slacks, and he produces a casino chip, a twinkle appearing in his eyes. The chip is green as his eyes and it has so many digits, I can hardly believe that a chip for this quantity exists.

"Meet my lucky coin, Mrs. Saint. Tahoe and Callan would kill for this beauty. I'm not going to cash it in until I take *you* to Dubai later in the year."

"Hmm. Bad call. You can't cash the lucky chip if it's *the* lucky chip."

He kisses my forehead. "I'll have *you* for luck."

I follow him as he rolls his suitcase back to the bedroom, drops his stuff, takes his passport out of his back pocket, takes off his watch and his shoes, and goes to turn on the shower. I set the lucky chip next to his passport, then lie back in bed and try not to imagine that the man of my every fantasy and dream is right now just a few feet away, naked and gloriously soaping himself up in the shower.

We're not supposed to have sex.

No. Sex.

Did you hear me, body?

God. Fuck this ridiculous idea.

But the wedding night will be utterly *perfect*!

Feeling right and safe again, I shift in bed. Our bed. It's too soft and comfortable. Suddenly I'm too afraid to fall asleep before I get to talk to him, so I transfer myself to a chair by the bedroom window and wait.

Head propped on my folded arm, I'm dreaming of us in Dubai when I hear familiar footsteps make their way out of the bathroom, out into the living room and kitchen, and then, a minute later, come back into the bedroom.

I'm achingly aware of the moment the footsteps finally come toward me. Before I know it, Malcolm slowly winds his arms under my legs and behind my back, picking me up to his chest. The smell of his warm skin lulls me more deeply toward sleep. He's warm. I can feel his heart beat through his bare chest. Thump. Thump. Strong. Resonating in my ears. I feel soft pillows beneath me.

His hands are now traveling up my calves. Slowly. Warm, callused fingers painting circles on my skin. Now they're at the backs of my knees. And his lips . . . are setting wandering little kisses on the inside of my knee.

I stir a little.

"Malcolm, we can't. I can't . . . I don't want to say no."

"Don't say no."

"Don't ask me."

His eyes glimmer in the shadows. "I'll just get *you* there tonight, then. I need my girl—the sounds she makes. The way she moves. The pink she gets."

As I look into his face, all the love I feel for him is like a fireball in my chest. "Did you get a lap dance?"

"No, I just watched dozens of naked women dance for me. Sent them over to lap-dance the poor fuckers who don't get what I do."

"Were they beautiful?"

He laughs a soft, dry rasp. "You're asking the most jaded eyes in town. They've seen lovelier. Every day they see something lovelier."

I feel like a teenager, so needy for his love. I can't have his body but I can have his love and I'll take that over anything.

I focus on his hands again, which are parting my thighs now. I feel the bed shift, and I open my eyes. He's kneeling between my legs. We make eye contact and I almost fall apart right there. His bare muscles look edible. His eyes look darker, a little scruff lining his jaw. The city lights play on his face, making him look hotter. Darker. Mysterious. Especially the way he is now, kneeling between my thighs, spreading them out farther, his eyes like storms, jaw clamped, hands rubbing up and down my thighs.

"That was the last time you get to . . . play," I warn.

"No, it's not. I play with you now." He's teasing, confident, and sexy. Then sober. "Missed you, Livingston." He reaches to the nightstand and I sit up, shocked to realize *why* he'd exited the bedroom moments ago as he picks up a can of whipped cream and urges, "Lean back."

I feel my heart hiccup. Skip a beat. And I squeeze my eyes shut. Holy god! All my other senses start amplifying. My shirt has ridden up to my waist now, my panties on full display. I feel that damned imaginary hand give a squeeze right below my belly button.

I lean back, as he asks.

His fingers are playing with the edges of my panties. Teasing. Rubbing. Painting his little circles. Stroking his thumbs back and forth beneath the sides of my panties. I'm breathing slightly harder now. I say slightly, but I fear my breath has become audible. A little laugh escapes my lips. The laugh turns into a gasp when I feel his lips skim against the top of one of my thighs. His hands are wandering over my legs. The backs of my knees, my inner thighs.

It's dangerous, how much I want him. Need him.

His lips are lovingly leaving little kisses across my thighs, slowly making their way up until he is kissing the little bow on the top of my panties. His hands push the shirt up higher, his mouth fixating on my belly button and giving it a little kiss. His warm hands mixed with his hot mouth slowly opening and closing on my skin gives me goose bumps. I feel my nipples harden, and Malcolm does not fail to notice.

"Keep your eyes closed," he murmurs, taking a breast and squeezing a little.

Heat explodes in my midsection.

Quivering, I lie here motionless.

"Malcolm, I didn't want to have one. A party, I mean. I didn't want some strange man near me. I definitely don't want anyone with whipped cream but you."

"Good. You have me. I'm all the man you're getting. And the one who's getting creamed is you."

He starts to unbutton the shirt of his I'm wearing, easing it off my shoulders to reveal my bare breasts. My legs still tingle from where he touched me. My insides feel like hot candle wax. He makes me want to melt. Combust. Explode.

I hear a sound and feel a little shock of cold in a perfect circle around my navel, and I'm dead. *Whipped fucking cream.* Around, and then into, my belly button.

His mouth kisses down my neck, toward the cream. Sucking on my skin, his tongue rubbing against my skin. Cue more goose bumps. And a rush of more when he tugs my panties down my legs.

His takes my knees and hooks my legs around his hips as he dips his head and starts lapping up the cream. I moan and grip his hair, loving the feel of it between my fingers.

I can feel his chest between my legs, right where I want him.

Where I want him and can't have him.

He takes my hands in his, our fingers interlacing, and he holds them at my sides. He's sucking on my abdomen. I feel like butter. My belly feels warm. I'm tingling all over. My head is turning to mush. I don't want to think—I *can't* think. He just feels so . . . good. Just so, so good. Gentle, firm mouth. Strong, smooth hands. Soft hair brushing against my breasts as he slowly trails his tongue upward.

I open my eyes, and when he looks at me, I see he's dying for it too. Just like I am.

"I can't wait to be inside you again," he growls softly. "My cock is jealous of my tongue and what it's about to do."

"Oh god, Saint, you're killing me."

"No, you're killing me. Little one, *you're* killing *me*. But the next time I'm inside you, you'll be my wife. Wife. I've got patience for you to spare." He kisses my mouth tenderly, and I gasp and pant. His body is buzzing with pent-up desire. Hunger of the kind that eats you up inside.

I can't move, don't stop him, don't breathe . . . I never breathe right when he touches me, when he's near.

He slides himself lower, slowly, making sure to rub between my legs, and I bite the inside of my cheek when he adds a healthy dose of whipped cream to my aching, throbbing, clenching wet sex. I shudder.

He looks ravenous when he bends his head and kisses me *there,* between my quaking thighs, and inside my body, and right up to my heart. His kiss is tender, possessive, completely breathtaking. He kisses completely. Takes everything I have. Leaves me breathless. I arch. Moan.

He groans and tightens his arms around me, his kiss deepening, his tongue thrusting mercilessly. He kisses me like that, over and over again. He tastes. Devours. Tasting me harder, deeper.

It's not the whipped cream he likes to taste, and I know it. He grows greedier when I'm sure there's no more whipped cream left . . . and only me. The way I want him.

Saint likes me like this, when I'm vulnerable and trusting him. And I'm a vulnerable mess right now. All noises and moaning and writhing.

He groans as I get wetter and wetter, my hips moving to the pleasure of his mouth. Turning to dust in his arms. I wrap my fingers around the back of his head, pressing him between my legs. His dark head moves, and he just kisses me, kisses the life out of me and tortures the hell out of himself as I climax on a hiss of breath, body bowing for him.

When he comes up, breathing harshly, every muscle is hard and flexed with need, taut from his denial.

I moan. "I want the whipped cream on you."

He kisses me. For a whole minute, his hands holding the back of my head, his mouth slow and leisurely savoring as he ducks his head over mine and sucks and nips and tastes, curling my toes.

Everything falls away.

I kiss him back, hungry, so very hungry for him *always*. I kiss him with my heart, my lips, with my mind, my hands on his shoulders, my soul.

"I agreed to wait until the wedding." His eyes twinkle with a devil's glint, but his jaw sets determinedly. "I hope you'll be ready for me."

I can't sleep. I'm anxious, excited. The wedding day feels so close now that Sin's home.

I nudge him in bed during the night, and he lifts a brow. "Hmm."

"Are you asleep?"

He rolls to his stomach and shoves his arm under his pillow, groaning. "Not anymore."

"You're jet-lagged. Go back to sleep. Sorry."

"Why are you not sleeping?"

"The invitations came in."

He looks at me as I steal away for a second, pull out the invitation, and show him the intertwined *M* and *R,* then the wording inside.

"Perfect," he says.

I smile and set it on the nightstand. "Do you think guests will keep a lid on it? Once the invites are out?"

He lifts his head and squints. Then drags a hand down his face. "No." He pulls me close. "We've got security anyway. No cameras, no press, no access, no anything."

"We can't stop them from speculating. Can we?" It's a waste of effort and energy to even try.

"No. We can't." He signals to my smartphone on the nightstand. "Whatever is in there . . . stays in there. Not here." He taps my brain. "Or here." He taps my heart. "All right?"

I nod.

"Go back to bed; you're jet-lagged." I slip my shoulder under his head and run my hands through his hair.

He turns and exhales near my neck. He kisses my forehead. Tightens his hold. "God, I missed you."

READY

Saint teased me on Whipped Cream Night. He wanted to know if I was ready.

I am so ready.

The fleet of M4 airplanes is ready.

Invitations are out.

Gifts are flowing in and they sit perfectly wrapped, waiting to be opened.

The invitations specify only the time and date we leave from O'Hare, and the date guests will be flown back. Apparently nobody is going to know where we're going beforehand.

Everything is set.

Malcolm Saint and I are getting married next weekend.

LEAKED

Secret wedding info leaked!

Speculation on magnate Malcolm Saint's marriage to reporter Rachel Livingston has simmered across the city. Sources confirm there has been a secret wedding scheduled at a very exclusive private island resort for sometime this month. No more than fifty close relatives, business associates, and friends will be in attendance.

More to come . . .

THE ISLAND

The M4 fleet of airplanes leaves early Wednesday to this perfect resort island, a favorite among celebrities. Private residences and beach bungalows occupy most of the land, along with a central resort hotel building where all cars arrive and depart from; the rest of the island is accessible only by golf carts, bicycles, or on foot.

Our reception will be held at the island botanical gardens, a mere three-minute walk from the chapel.

When the fleet of M4 airplanes land, Saint, my mother, and I emerge from one of the planes. Another brings Tahoe, Callan, and a dozen of Saint's friends. Another flies in Wynn, Gina, Valentine, Sandy, and my old *Edge* colleagues. One more carries Saint's business acquaintances. A handful more fly in our security and wedding crew.

Everyone is impressed by the lush surroundings and the deliciously warm breeze because Malcolm Saint and I are getting married in *paradise.*

"Wow." Tahoe strides over and slaps Malcolm's back, his Texan drawl coming out. "You did good, man."

Saint laughs and slaps him back. "Tell me something new."

PLAYING AT THEBEACH

We're sleeping in side-by-side presidential suites overlooking the water.

Our guests occupy the rest of the resort, all of them in bungalows, save for my mother and friends, who want to be near me for preparations the day of the wedding. The hotel staff has treated us like kings and queens since arrival, which makes sense given that Saint booked the whole island for us—our guests, the security, photographers, and chefs are the only ones here.

Sin has been spending every day since we landed with me, but when night comes, I end up alone in my suite, sometimes inviting my mother or Gina over so that I'm not tempted to sleepwalk—awake—and end up knocking on his door.

Nights feel eternal, but between travel, getting settled, and the last of the wedding preparations, the days have flown by so fast, I can hardly believe that tomorrow, at last, is the wedding.

Tomorrow we wed.

We wed, and then bed. *Yes!*

The girls have gone bike riding. My mother has been reading in her room. Saint and I spend our last free day on the island together, drinking Bloody Marys (me) and Aviator gin (him), diving into the waves and then lying out in the sun to get warm.

The sky is orange as the sun sets right now. I'm wet enough that my fingers are crinkled and as I float in the water, too tired to swim, I'm pretty sure I see a flat, dark-colored moving object swim beside me.

I freeze, hold my breath as it passes.

"Malcolm, there's a stingray. Right here, it just grazed me. *Holy shit!*"

I hurry out of the water, and instead of swimming away he dives into the water and swims forward, and after it.

He comes back up. "It's a banded guitarfish."

"Well, why are you following it?"

He laughs and slicks his hair back as he swims forward and comes to his feet. "It's harmless, Rachel."

I drop into the sand, clutching the towel to my chest. Sunlight gleams in his eyes as if it's being reflected in water.

He wades out of the waves.

"You have no respect for predators," I chide. "You're absolutely irreverent. How do you even know it's that kind of fish, Dr. Aquatics?"

"Snorkeling across the world. Swimming with sharks. The adrenaline, Rachel." He shoots me a devil-may-care smirk.

My heart starts thudding, my mouth running dry. I miss him terribly. I miss the way his body talks to mine. The way he loves me with his hands and mouth.

His wet swim trunks cling to his powerful hips and thighs as he comes over; he looks powerful but fluid, chest broad and muscular, and agile. He is a man whose muscles were built testing out his thirst for adrenaline.

He drops down beside me, stretches his legs out, props himself up on his elbows, and gazes at the sky. I study the sky too, but only for a minute. I find the sight of him more interesting; in fact, I always seem to find myself constantly trying to read his thoughts. I study his confident profile and notice his mouth is curved humorously.

His head swings lazily to the side and he looks at me with a slightly rising eyebrow. Then he reaches out and strokes the damp tendrils from my face. It's only one touch. One tiny touch of his two fingers on my hair. Strong, warm, familiar, and a little wet. A long, pleasant shiver overtakes me.

He just smiles, and I'm clinging desperately to my responsible, sensible self, who knows we will only have one, one, wedding night.

"Don't seduce me, Sin." I lift the towel so he can't see how hard my nipples have gotten.

"Me?" He lifts his hands devilishly, a mischievous spark in his eye. "I've done nothing yet. Nothing that I really wanted to do."

I feel my skin color. "You have that glint in your eye, Saint. I want the perfect wedding night with you."

"And you're going to get it."

"So why are you leaning forward?"

He lifts his hand. "I'm pretending I don't know what it feels like to do this." He eases his fingers under my hair and plays with it naturally, casually.

I close my eyes and feel relaxation spreading through me. I try not to moan. "Good. Focus on that."

"I can't. I need some self-control not remembering what it's like to nibble your ears. Right here. Where it drives me crazy."

Dizzy with anticipation and excitement, I shiver.

"You like having your fun, don't you?" I mock him playfully.

"I like having fun with my girl."

"With me, or making fun of me and my wish for a perfect wedding night?"

He's hard and I'm wet and we're panting.

"What makes it perfect is you and me. I could have you ten times tonight and want you as much tomorrow."

"All the women in my life have advised otherwise."

"As the only man in your life, I strongly disagree," he says, but seems to put the matter aside in good humor.

"I bet you do."

When he laughs, he sounds so boyish. His laugh breaks off, and his eyes start to smolder with something beyond lust, and more like *need*. We stare at each other: Every time our eyes lock, I want his taste in my mouth.

He's looking at me hotly.

As if he wants more than to taste.

He reaches out and tugs the knot at the nape of my neck. "I miss the sight of you."

My bikini top unravels.

I reach for it.

"Don't," he gruffly commands.

His eyes lazily rove over me, like a feather's touch on my skin.

He brushes a finger over the back of my neck, touching my body as naturally as he breathes. "You're blushing." He runs a finger down my cheek. Gone in a second. His eyes flick up to mine, and then he's looking at me with an intense and secret expression. "By the time you let me have you again, you'll be blushing even deeper."

"Enjoy it while it lasts. The blushes. I can't be a blushing old lady."

"I rather hope you will be."

"Nope. I need to be a composed old lady."

"I'll do my best to decompose my old lady as frequently as I can."

God, I have a desperate urge to kiss his devil-sucks-my-dick-every-night smile.

Unable to resist, I kiss his lips, quickly, and feel him pat my ass as he gets up and we head for our rooms. "Decompose me after the wedding."

"I'm planning to do much more than that."

As we gather our towels, he looks at me and says, "Hey, I sent something to your room."

My eyes widen. "What?"

"Why do you look so uncomfortable when I get you something?"

"I'm not used to it."

He frowns. "I need to work on that."

"Not you, I need to."

"I plan to spoil you, Miss Saint . . . often."

"I'm going to let you."

He stares down at me with heated eyes. "Good."

"And spoil you right back."

"Have fun with it."

"With what? Spoiling you?"

"That too."

"Oh. My *gift*! What is it? A vibrator?"

He frowns. "Why would I want anything inside you other than me?" He tsks and taps a fingertip playfully to my temple. "This abstinence isn't doing you good, Livingston."

VISIT BEFORE THE WEDDING

In my room I find four dresses.

The Vera Wang, Reem Acra, Yumi Katsura, and Monique Lhuillier—two of them even include handwritten notes from the designers themselves.

From simple, to Regency style, to one covered in what looks like diamond dust, these are the most beautiful dresses I've ever seen—the finest for his girl. I feel warm just thinking about him having a hand in making sure they were ready for our day.

I touch the materials, then I spend the next hour trying them on.

They're so spectacular, each one as pretty as the last. I wouldn't even know which to pick!

But no.

I think I've set my fear aside. I'm getting married with his mother's engagement ring and my mother's dress.

As I take off the last dress, Gina, Wynn, and my mother are all oohing and aahing in my living room.

"He spoils you, girl!" Gina says laughing.

But Wynn and Mom are *gushing*.

I remember my mother reading about love languages. After my father died, she wanted to be sure that I felt loved as a child, so she read books, went to conferences, and explained to me that people express love in different ways. She said there were five basic ways, which include: touch, gifts, service to your loved ones, quality time together, and verbal feedback. Not everyone responds to, or uses, the same language, which can cause miscommunication in relationships.

Touch was my language. She was told to be tender, and she *was*. I responded well to her hugs. I simply respond *well* to physical contact.

I can't explain, even on the evening before my wedding, how good and perfect it feels when Saint holds the back of my head in one hand and my entire back in the other and kisses me. I think Sin's love language is touch too. But also gift giving—this man is *relentless* when it comes to showering me with amazing things!

While the girls and Mother help put each dress back into its protective cover, I head into the adjoining bedroom to change.

I slip into Saint's large, white button shirt, a pair of leggings, and my socks, then I pull open the glass doors and step out to feel the breeze and get some fresh night air. Through the crashing of the waves, I hear the guys talking in the private patio. My skin crackles pleasurably as I hear Saint's baritone.

". . . reason both you and Gina didn't bring dates to the wedding . . . ?" Malcolm's tone is cool and quiet, but there's an underlying threat of caution in his words.

A full-on silence that follows, broken only by Tahoe's quiet "Really? I hadn't noticed."

"Gina. Now there's a lady who goes down as smoothly as an

abrasive," Callan says.

"Stay away, T. She's Rachel's best friend." This from Saint. No nonsense, and kind of exasperated.

Tahoe stays quiet.

The silence stretches, and then comes the sound of what seems like ice cubes being pulled out of the chiller.

"When you saw Rachel for the first time, what did you feel?" Tahoe asks, low.

"Felt new. I felt like I saw a woman for the first time."

Oh my god. I'm fluttering to my toes.

"Yeah. That's not how I feel," Tahoe says.

"You're just irked that she hasn't thrown her underwear at your head," Callan lazily deduces.

"Fucking pissed."

"Pissed that she'd rather have anyone else than you and your billions." Callan keeps on expertly rubbing it.

"Absolutely ludicrous, but there you have it."

"She'd rather be your friend than be in your bed."

"Motherfuck me, yes," Tahoe growls.

I get that little squeeze right in the center of my tummy when Saint's voice floats up to me next. "She's a good girl, T. The kind you play house with, not games."

"Fucking relax, Saint. I won't do anything you wouldn't do."

There's a soft laugh. "Touché."

I turn back to the living room and realize the girls are wide-eyed, especially Gina. Could she hear them, too, through the open doors? An amused smile touches my lips, and I grab my phone from the bed and text Malcolm:

We heard you
Just thought you should know

Gina looks like she just swallowed a little bit of wire

Shortly he replies:

Sorry
He's had a bottle of Pinot
U going to sleep any time soon?

Me: Too excited to

Saint: You miss me?

Me: A little

Saint: Text me when you miss me a little more

Me: Oh don't wait up! Enjoy the booze and the boys. I know how HARDcore you are

Saint: How well you know me

I smile at the phone. And ache in all sorts of places. I write, I do miss you. Perfect wedding night seems more impossible by the second, but I'm determined

Saint: It'll be perfect

Me: So don't tempt me, SIN!

Saint: I want my girlfriend in my arms, our last night together

Oh, fuck him and the Saint Effect. My butterflies are flapping, so awake right now I can hardly stand steady enough to text: I want my boyfriend too. Tell him to come over before he goes to sleep. He's been the best boyfriend I've ever had. He should get one last kiss.

He replies simply, I can taste you already.

The guys keep talking with lowered voices. Heading back to the living room to drop myself on a couch, I pop my phone into the stereo and play soft music so the girls don't overhear anymore.

Gina's super thoughtful, though.

She's spread out, all her voluptuous curves hugged by the extra-long T-shirt she wears. She's like Marilyn Monroe in brunette, and now very quiet. Wynn's hair is spread out behind her on the other side of the couch. My friends are both pretty, young, and sprightly. But no match for Saint's friends.

Callan and Tahoe are attractive and unscrupulous enough to take *any* woman without a thought.

"Four dresses, that's . . . unheard-of," I hear Wynn say as her eyes drift back to the four designer dresses hanging in their plastic coverings. "What's your language, Rache?" Wynn asks.

My attention snaps back to the group, and it takes me only a second to catch on to what she means. "Words for sure." *Dibs!* "Touch, too."

"I am so touch. In fact if we go an hour together and Emmett hasn't held my hand, I'm convinced he's stopped loving me."

Gina shakes her head and curls her legs beneath her. "I don't trust words. Touch makes me uncomfortable. But I'll take the gifts."

I wag my head no. "That's not your love language, Gina. You service others. You put food in the fridge. You look out for them."

"If a guy does that for you, and speaks to you in your looooove language," Wynn warns, "you'll be toast. Buttery hot toast."

"No problem, since most guys are selfish. They want to be serviced, not the other way around."

"They're like us, Gina," Wynn counters. "Except with a lot of sexy testosterone. Which, thanks to the abstinence, will have skyrocketed by the time Rachel reaches the honeymoon. I can feel Saint; he's just a tad pissy with Tahoe. He's sexually frustrated. He wants you, Rachel."

I think I feel it too and I'm speeding a thousand miles an hour on the highway to heaven.

"What you can feel is our girl's pre-wedding hormones gone crazy."

I hug my pillow and grin so hard, pressing the pillow against my body and all the aching places, my nipples, between my legs, even my stomach, which is whirling. "I shall not apologize for lusting after my fiancé. Everybody else does it, and I get to do it for the rest of my life, which is pretty damn fine to me."

The heat of our bodies. The pull is so strong between us, even in silence we seem to communicate.

I can't wait to melt into the protectiveness of his arms.

How I feel wistful and relaxed when close to him. This comfort of being close—his presence so male, strong. Every fiber of my being aches. I let my mind drift off to our wedding night. The almond oil, sweet smelling and glistening, that I plan to wear on my skin. The La Perla bra and panties, perfect lace, perfectly see-through, that I plan to wear on my sexy parts . . .

I realize then that Gina is really withdrawn and unusually quiet. "What's happened with Tahoe, Gina?" I ask softly.

"Nothing. We're friends. We . . . I guess we talk. A lot."

"What about?"

"Things."

"Paul?"

"I told him about Paul."

Disbelief widens my eyes. "You did! Babe, that's huge for you! To open up like that to a guy."

"He's a friend. He's a great listener, actually. But I don't really want to talk about that now." She spreads out my veil a little more. "How did you choose your wedding dress?" Gina then asks. "And the veil?"

"It's as hard as choosing the groom, I bet," Wynn says.

"Actually no. They both chose me. I was afraid of both . . . a little. But I'm sure he's the one." I point at my mom's dress and my mother's eyes instantly widen. "And that's the one."

"Really?" Mother asks.

"Really. I'm sure."

"It's a sexy dress, Mama," Wynn gushes. "I wish my mom had that cleavage. Your Saint is going to think all devil thoughts while in church. Another benefit to . . . abstinence!"

"Abstinence!" they all cheer.

"Easy for you to say, but revenge will be sweet. I'll be the one wrapping the chastity belts around *you* two before your wedding days."

"Gina's chastity belt is her mouth, she opens it and the guys run. Except Tahoe."

Gina shoots Wynn a withering look. "He's my bud. You two don't get to talk evil about him."

"Well, Gina, one day . . ." my always-optimistic mother says.

"It's nice to imagine it, that it's out there. Doing more is hard, though. I can imagine it, I can see it, and I *like* seeing it. I just don't want to pull back the curtain with my name on it and find out I'm the one who picked the losing card. I'd rather . . . imagine there was something wonderful in store."

"There could be," Mother insists.

"Maybe. But right now, it's enough to think that there could be. I'm not ready to find out that there isn't."

We're tired enough to run out of talk but too wired to sleep. The girls propose watching a wedding movie. *"My Best Friend's Wedding?"* I ask as I scroll through the offerings on the hotel pay-per-view.

"You've seen that one a gazillion times. Let's watch Steve Martin. This one is fun. Fun, Rachel. Really," says Wynn.

"I don't know. *Father of the Bride* . . . Mom?" I ask my mother uncertainly.

It's a movie I've always shied away from simply because . . . well, my father isn't here.

My mother wavers a little bit, an instant of worry on her face, but then she looks at my friends' faces and the hopeful look I wear—a look that might say I want her to tell me I am strong enough to watch it. I'm happy, I'm older, I'm good.

"It's a beautiful movie," my mom finally says before she heads off to her room, to bed.

Pacified, I click the purchase button, cross the room, close the open windows, and settle in bed to watch it with my friends.

It starts perfect. Proposal. Funny, jealous dad. The parts where he is acting a little nutty and protective make the corners of my eyes start to leak. Soon, the dam breaks. And I'm a waterfall.

"Oh no!" Wynn pauses the movie. "Gina, look for *My Best Friend's Wedding.*"

Before she can hug me and I start getting truly emotional, I leap to my feet and hide in the bathroom, washing my face for a long time.

Wynn knocks. "You okay? Saint's at the door."

I look at my face, and thank goodness my eyes haven't swelled up. Thanks, three minutes of cold water. I tie my hair in a bun and realize, with a little kick of adrenaline—he wants *his kiss*! So I quickly wash my mouth with Scope.

All the things that happen to me physically when I see him are already poised to take over when I swing open the door, bend down to set the door stopper so I'm not shut out, and step outside.

His strong, deliciously unique energy envelops me like a cloak.

"The guys aren't letting up anytime soon," he explains to me softly when I just stand there and drink in the sight of him like a junkie.

He's in lounge pants and a soft V-neck T-shirt, the fabric draping over his hard body and delineating every muscle. Between his lashes, his eyes are resting hungrily on me. As if he misses the sight of me.

"Neither are the girls." I wipe my cheek again to make sure no tears remain.

He smiles wryly and props a shoulder on the wall, and then he studies me curiously, as if he can see the tears still on my cheeks. "Thought I'd claim my kiss before it felt like a good-morning one," he says softly.

"It's already morning anyway." I grin up at him. "But I'll give you a day kiss tomorrow in my wedding dress."

His fingers curve under my chin. "So . . . which are you wearing?"

God, my heart is swooning inside. His bold, handsome face smiles warmly down at me. I can't wait for him to see me in white. Walking up to him, ready and eager to become his wife.

"Do you want to picture me?" I probe, smiling happily as the look in his eyes tells me that he *does*. I'm smiling fully now, happiness spreading inside me. "You haven't seen the one I'll be wearing."

His warm fingers curl around my jaw and he turns my head as if he means to kiss me, but instead, he just keeps smiling. "I can't wait to make you my lady. Your smiles drive me crazy."

"I missed you."

His lips curl even higher, tenderly so. "Are you nervous?"

I nod. "But . . . excited."

His chiseled face is still softened by his smile as he strokes his thumb from one edge of my smile to the other. "I overestimated myself thinking I could wait longer to marry you."

I nod and stay quiet, feeling the weight of his gaze on me, which suddenly makes me feel like my heart just burst open. "We were watching *Father of the Bride* and I was bawling like a baby." I duck my head into his shirt and start bawling again.

"Come here." He presses me against the flat of his chest, and I fist a handful of shirt and speak into the fabric that smells clean and deliciously like him.

"I don't know why I'm crying. It's a funny movie. I was laughing."

He grabs his phone and shoots off a text. "Come here." He wraps an arm around my waist and I struggle to stop crying as he leads me to the elevators.

"Where are we . . . ?"

"They're getting us a room."

We descend to the lobby, where Otis stands ready at the elevator bank. Saint steps out and holds the doors open as Otis hands him a key. Saint steps back in, presses the button for the tenth floor, and then pulls me back into his arms as we ride upstairs.

We head into the junior suite, and then he leads me out to the terrace, where there are a set of chaises and a table with four chairs, and a view of the water.

He lowers himself onto a chaise and pulls me down with him. He stretches his long legs and I shift above him, then cuddle close as he dries my tears. "I miss my dad right now. Because it's something a dad does. Protect his family. Not all of them. But some."

He looks into my face, then he draws his lips thoughtfully. "I remember that movie. I'd make sure our girl made a smart choice before I handed her off to some bastard."

"Sin!" I laugh when I realize he already sounds annoyed and jealous. "When I go back in there, I'm going to picture you as the dad. And it'll be perfect. It'll be funny now."

He laughs.

His arm clutches me just a little tighter, almost tight enough to make it hard to breathe. And all the emptiness of the old is replaced by the fullness of the new. I lie there against him, enjoying the soft brushing of his fingers against my cheek.

"Would you ever forgive him? Your own father?"

He laughs softly, then his laugh trails off. "No." He frowns and shakes his head, his eyes a little bit threatening. "I'm not good at forgiveness."

"You forgave *me*."

"I understood why you did it. You were doing your job. I'd do my job before anything else. That was me too. I understood that . . . this"—brows drawn low, he swings a finger between us—"took you by surprise. It took *me* by surprise how much anything on the media could fuck me up when Victoria's reveal leaked."

I'm glad we can talk about it now. I'm glad it's starting to get exorcised out of both of us.

"I will never again be on anyone's team but yours; you know that, don't you? Unless of course if we argue, because I'll probably be arguing about a good point and you'll be too stubborn to admit it. Maybe I'll be trying to make you see that our little girl's boyfriend is a good guy."

"He fucking better be."

I grin and set my face back on his chest, and think of us. How we began quietly, like most storms. We began actually under a sunny sky. But the clouds in our sky built steadily into a thunderhead. When the sun came back out, what was left behind was not what had been there before. Now it's better after the rain; at least it feels like so much more.

He shifts me above him so that we're both facing the waves and the horizon. He signals at the sky. "Where we're going on our honeymoon, we'll be able to see every speck up there."

Smiling, I glance back over my shoulder and peer into his face. "Somewhere?"

Beneath my spine, his chest rumbles from a chuckle, causing my head to feel swimmy. "That's right."

"The office thing under control?"

His voice tickles the back of my ear. "We get four days off, no phones. After that I can't promise."

"Four is a lot. What will we talk about?" I frown thoughtfully at the water.

"You. Me. Us. Our apartment. This ear." He tugs the ear. I laugh and turn to him again.

He exchanges a smile with me, then we lay there for another hour, just talking and gazing at a sky whose stars are partly hidden by the lights down on earth.

He holds my hand as he walks me to the door of my suite. I feel like a teen, waiting to see if she'll be kissed. Knowing she can't go in *without* a kiss. He looks at my mouth, then his eyes come up to study my face intently. Deep in thought.

"Your kiss," I say, because I know he wants it.

I stand on my toes, the heels of my palms resting on his chest for balance.

He kisses the corner of my mouth and takes me by the waist, groaning softly, his eyes fluttering closed for one second. Only one. Before they open with steely determination. "If you kiss me, it'll kill me." His eyes blaze. "I'm fresh out of patience, trying to make your wedding night perfect." He smiles ruefully.

"Saint, thank you for being so understanding and patient."

He tweaks my ear. "I'll make you pay tomorrow."

A delicious shiver of want runs through me. "With interest."

"Worst rate in the market."

"I love you," I say before he can leave.

"Love you too." He rumples my hair. "Go out there and live the single life." He pats my butt.

"Like it's so fun compared to what's in store . . ." I tease.

He smiles and watches me go inside with a twinkle in his eye and a pure smile, as if I'm already perfect for him.

THE BIGDAY

The next morning is a flurry of makeup, hair, manicure, and pedicure. I'm in my underwear, ready to start putting on the dress, the lace tiara, and the veil when Gina arrives.

"Half of the hotel staff is swooning in the lobby, I swear to god," she says.

I feel a jealous twinge at the thought that others have been able to see my groom before me. "Who?"

"Receptionists, florists, waitresses, everyone with a vagina. Women were sitting down fanning themselves. *Swear*." She laughs and then shoots me a deathly sober look that says *I kid you not!*

"Where are the rings?" I ask her.

"Hey, don't look at me. I'm not supposed to bring them, Tahoe is."

"He better bring them along with his hangover after the rehearsal dinner."

She grabs her phone. "T-Rex, don't forget the rings or we'll have a bridezilla on our hands."

"We?" asks Wynn, where she still sits by the breakfast cart that room service had brought up.

"What?"

"You just said 'we,' " says Wynn.

"Ah, whatever." Gina comes over and mothers me.

Wynn is eyeing the other dresses as she eats a piece of toast. "Are all these going back?" she asks. "I mean . . . they're huge designers. And they sent *notes*!"

"I don't think they're going back," I say as Mother holds open the dress for me to step into.

"If I need an emergency wedding . . ." Wynn trails off.

"No period yet?" I ask worriedly.

Wynn is a week late.

She told us last night after I came to the room to find *her* crying a little bit.

"None. But it's all the stress and excitement of your wedding. Plus travel always messes with my cycle." Convinced she's nailed the problem, she fishes out a bagel from the bread basket and bites down.

"Right," says Gina. "Does Emmett even want kids?"

Wynn has no response for that.

Gina shoots her a meaningful look. "Guess you should ask."

"Really? Is that what *we* think?" Wynn shoots back.

"What *I* think."

Mom has buttoned up the sides of my low-back dress, and I am momentarily left speechless by the image in the mirror hanging on the back of the en suite bathroom door. I take in the milky color of my skin, the pink of my cheeks. The dress is formfitting with a low back and a little bit of cleavage and a mermaid skirt, emphasizing my waist and hips, and even my small breasts. My hair hangs like a curtain behind me, and   it looks lustrous as glass. My mother adds the tiara to the crown of my head and attaches the veil, letting the rear hang delicately over my backside, and the short one to cover my face.

She holds the purple orchids that I'm supposed to carry, and stares at me with tears in her eyes.

Wynn and Gina stop arguing, and they catch their breath when I turn. "So you like it?" I ask them.

This is the one dress they hadn't seen on me.

And once they see it, they get misty eyes too.

"No crying," I plead, my heart suddenly feeling like a thousand pounds in my chest.

I'm too excited to cry. I'm too happy to marry my Saint. I'm too determined not to have *puffy eyes*.

"No crying," Gina softly concurs as she goes and takes the bagel from Wynn's hand and slaps it down on the plate. "We have a wedding to take her to. Her player will be a player no more; he just got himself a missus."

Down in the lobby, the hotel staff is waiting in a neat line to greet me. "Congratulations! You make a beautiful bride. Oh, and your friend was just here. She worried she was already late for the wedding but we assured her she was just on time."

"Friend?" I ask quizzically.

I glance behind me, where Gina and Wynn stand along with Mother. Do they mean Sandy? Valentine? I mean to ask, but then I spot a familiar person ducking with her arm raised to cover her face. I spot a bun, and an executive outfit like some paparazzi pro. For a moment my body stiffens at the shock of seeing her. Pretty as you damn well please. But the shock gives way to indignation and protectiveness. I purse my lips in anger,

I lift my skirts, and walk over.

"Victoria." I stop her.

She freezes, turns, and gets this "oh-my-god-you-here?" look on her face. "Hey, Rachel."

"What are you doing here?"

"I, well, there were rumors. I'm representing the people."

"She's like a bloodhound sniffing them out!" Gina cries.

"You've got some nerve," Wynn huffs. "We're calling Saint."

"Wynn, no," I say, reaching out to stop her.

I step aside and pull Victoria along with me.

"Rachel, I won't do any harm. I'm so sorry for what happened," she says.

"No," I say. "You're sorry my boyfriend canned your article and got you out of a job."

"No!" Her eyes widen. "I *like* this job. I'm like Perez Hilton on Twitter. I'm free; I like it. I have you and him to thank." She lifts her phone. "One picture?"

"You're kidding me," I say, outraged.

"Press can't come in, cameras controlled, but I'm not press, see, not officially; my phone does the trick, please. I know your single name, and described you . . . so. I mean, we *are* friends."

"Were," I whisper, then I try to calm myself. "Please leave."

We stare at one another.

She was someone I wanted to be like.

But I don't anymore.

She has her path and I have mine.

I don't want to hate her either.

And I don't think she hates me. In fact, I see regret in her eyes. She bows her head in shame and wrings her hands as she presses her phone to her chest. "Rachel, I'm sorry. For what it's worth." She looks contrite. "I saw him walk past." She signals. "You're lucky." I don't reply, and she adds, as if to make me feel better, "So is he."

"You still need to leave, Victoria."

There seems to be a battle inside her. The professional versus the human being. "I'll go because I owe you one. But I'll see you at the christening of your firstborn, or maybe sooner."

I smile at her naïveté. This is the last time she slips by me. "I don't think so," I say.

She smiles a little and walks away. And I watch her take my past with her, all of it.

I have a future to look forward to.

I have a storm to catch.

A leap to make.

A man to love.

A Sin to take.

And I've never looked forward to something in my life like I look forward to

MALCOLM

KYLE

PRESTON

LOGAN

SAINT.

WEDDING

There's only one chapel on the island, and it's barely a year old. When the original one suffered a fire, one of the billionaires who frequently vacations here had a new one made. The architecture is exquisite, with thick columns and high arches, old mosaics gracing the windows, brought here from antiques shops and auction blocks from across the world. The altar is all white marble, with sculptures hiding in strategically positioned nooks, as well as frescoes on the painted ceiling, reminiscent of Michelangelo.

Today the chapel feels like a garden.

I know this because I came to look at it yesterday, and I know that a waterfall of white orchids hangs over the altar. I know that the aisle rows are dripping with more orchids that trail down to the long red carpet. I know that there are thousands of warmly lit candles awaiting behind the massive antique doors, and that the chorus is accompanied by one of Chicago's finest orchestras, all flown down here for the wedding.

I can't breathe in this dress. I CAN'T BREATHE knowing that he's waiting for me. Behind these doors. Down that freshly cleaned, red-carpeted aisle. Up on the luminous white marble altar and under the hanging orchids. My *groom*.

Every part of me shakes. Quakes. *Aches.*

Sandy and Valentine waited outside, and they're helping Gina and Mom spread out my veil to make sure I look perfect.

Perfect.

Please, please, god, let me look perfect.

We will only marry once. He will only watch me once. And I'm burning for him to burn for me like I do him.

There are days meant to be perfect in your life. So ethereal and mystical. I hadn't dared imagine this one, though. First, because I didn't want it . . . never knew I wanted it. Next, because I wanted it so very much.

And now the day is upon me and upon him.

My hair falls behind me, a plain veil covering my face, my wedding dress fitting like it had been made for me. Outside the wind is warm and perfect. The cathedral is bathed in white. The doors swing open. I hear the chorus start.

The air rushes through me, electric, excited, as alive as I feel. I watch my friends walk before me. They look like exotic birds from overseas. I'm in white, my favorite color. It didn't used to be my favorite, until I met him. He is so dark, and makes me feel so bright and light in return. The air between us solidifies. I see him. He sees me.

His eyes laser through the thin veil, and I feel charged by green fire. Green fire flowing in my veins. Green fire fiery in my stomach.

And then, he smiles.

Kaboom goes my heart.

I have no fears.

No regrets.

Only a rush of happiness so pure, it hurts in my chest. Tears of emotion start filling my eyes; my mother's arm is trembling in mine. And I realize she has a trail of tears, happy tears to match the smile on her face.

Through my tears I keep looking ahead to the black, tall, regal shape of my groom. Watching me, intent, his hands clasped before him, his shoulders straight, his legs braced apart, as I walk up.

The future father of all my little Saints, though I'm prepared for devils, the whole lot of them.

And walking up to him feels like the rightest thing I've ever done in my life.

I don't want him to see me cry again.

I want to wipe my tears, but I'm afraid to snag the veil. I will tell him, later, that I'm crying because I'm happy. He makes me so happy. My chest swells as we approach; he becomes larger, darker, clearer to my eyes, and oh so very and extremely perfect.

I'm hazy with anticipation when Mom hands me over to Saint.

He takes my hand in his warm, strong grip, and his smile never leaves his face, not for a second.

In a rush, heat eats up my body.

He's staring at me through my veil, his face blurry through the material. Slowly he lifts the lace, and a look like summer lightning brightens his eyes when he sees me. He sees my tears then, and his gaze fills with an endless tenderness that blooms in my heart. He dries me slowly with his thumbs, and I take one of his big hands in mine and kiss the center of his palm, my kiss saying that *he* is the center of my world now.

His answer is exquisite.

One sole ghost kiss. Right on the corner of my mouth, where my smile goes, then he draws me up to his side, and I follow him up the two steps, breathing as he breathes, moving as he moves, onto the altar.

Malcolm Kyle Preston Logan Saint. My first everything. The man who woke me up. The man who made my world spin faster, the wind feel colder, grapes taste sweeter than ever. Amplified all my senses and left me *alive, breathing*—so when I messed up, I felt it more than ever.

And now here we are.

I am marrying this beautiful, ambitious, intelligent, generous, caring man, who holds me close, has always kept me close, even when he was so angry at me.

There is no closeness that surpasses where we're going. Nothing more intimate. More precious than he can give me, and I him.

I pass my bouquet to Gina and Wynn fidgets with the long veil behind me.

The ceremony begins—dreamlike and musical. I absorb the chorus, the priest's words, the man beside me. Tahoe hands us the rings.

Malcolm slips the ring onto my finger. "I give you this ring as a token of my love." His smile is all tender and male. He watches me intently as I slip the thicker band onto his left hand, our fingers lacing together.

The priest proceeds to where I will finally vow to *take this man*.

My mouth dries up. I look up at Malcolm and try to speak as clearly as I can, my stomach warmed by the loving way he looks at me.

"I, Rachel, take you, Malcolm, to be my lawfully wedded husband, my friend, my partner, and my love from this day forward. In the presence of god, our family, and friends, I offer you my solemn vow to be your faithful partner in sickness and in health, in good times and in bad, and in joy as well as in sorrow. I promise to love you unconditionally, to support you in your goals, to honor and respect you, and to cherish you for as long as we both shall live." I'm breathless as I finish, and I smile a little. There's a gleam of intensity and hunger in his eyes as he listens to me.

When the priest begins to say, "You may now kiss—"

Saint kisses me. He puts one arm around my waist and squeezes me affectionately, and then he lifts me by the waist, up to his mouth, to kiss me longer and harder.

The music soars, "Ode to Joy" as we walk out of the church as man and wife.

SIN AND SINNER

Buzzfeed.com
#SAINT VS. SINNER

Malcolm Saint's legendary and controversial girlfriend is causing quite a stir as we get wind of a snippet of the prenup to her now-husband, who put the rush on their upcoming nuptials by tying the knot on a secluded island last Saturday. Apparently the prenup enforces a strict loyalty clause if our favorite manwhore strays—and he's betting his money on the fact that he won't. The clause is equally demanding of Mrs. Saint. The exact sums and punishments are not known, as Saint is known to guard his private matters with his wife zealously. Which makes us more determined to find out . . .

Updates from @VictoryVictoria on Twitter:

Respecting the couples wish for privacy so no o pics from the
Saint wedding, Twitterville, sorry!!!

But I can confirm the wedding took place earlier today!

The bride wore a vintage dress with decadent cleavage

The groom made angels siiiiiiiigh

I will say . . . congratulations to the pair!

Who to stalk while the honeys are mooning around the world?

@VictoryVictoria Imagine @malcolmsaint on his honeymoon,
OH MY WOW

@VictoryVictoria Definitely a hornymoon if Saint's involved. Or
WHORNYMOON

Wonder how long it'll last.

SOMEWHERE

We fly all day across the Pacific, toward a little island near Bali he rented for us alone. At first, when we board the Gulfstream, the adrenaline is running through my veins. I'm reliving the teary farewells from my friends, the hard slaps on the back Saint got from his friends, and my mother's hug.

I can't stop reliving any of the things that happened at the wedding.

We partied across the botanical gardens, decorated in hanging tree lights and more white orchids, tables draped in crisp white linens, Tiffany chairs, and Christofle silverware. We dined on a five-course meal worthy of the finest restaurant—and *catered* by one—and then Malcolm pulled me to the dance floor and into his arms, guests floating around us as we laughed, and drank, and kissed, and stayed close.

He embraced me from behind as we conversed with our guests. "Twenty-four hours," he whispered in my ear.

"What's that?"

He brushed a strand of hair back and pulled my back closer against him. "Wedding party, plus the flight to Somewhere. Twenty-four hours left for me to make you mine."

Now I'm in his arms, on the big bed in the bedroom at the back of the plane. Sunlight streams through the windows as Saint kisses me.

His hands are under my lace top, slipping to touch my skin. I'm seared where he touches. Where his mouth lands. On my mouth, the corners of my mouth, my jaw, my ears, my neck.

"Can it be night already?" I whisper.

"Rachel . . ." and the word is a husky murmur as he eases back to look at me. So hungry, like me. So very frustrated I can feel his need for me like I feel mine. He kisses the corner of my mouth. "I'm not taking my wife for the first time on an airplane. That's for later." He flashes out a grin that liquefies me. But I know he knows that the moment we walk through the doors of our Somewhere, I will be all *his*.

"Come here." Malcolm spoons me and buries his head in the back of my neck, his arm a vise around my hip. A bottomless peace and satisfaction fill me as our bodies fit together so right, my body covered by his bigger one. It feels perfect, like a clean room. A finished job. An orgasm. God, a cataclysmic orgasm, like the kind this man gives me. My . . . husband.

He's wearing the wedding ring I gave him, on his long, tanned, strong finger, glinting in perfect platinum as he holds his hand on my hip.

I doze to sleep with a throbbing, relentless ache in my body but a smile in my heart and on my face, and we sleep, and sleep, and then shift positions—him on his back, me on my side, spooning his side, and we sleep again.

We land in a tiny airport that's hardly an airport at all,   but there's a beautiful car waiting for us, driving us across unpaved paths into the middle of nowhere. It starts raining. One minute there's sun, the next there's a storm. I reject the idea as absurd—it's not in the plan—but then I look out the car window. The heavens suddenly open up and a torrential downpour starts. My dormant brain cells wake up a little when thunder crashes nearby.

Fuuck!

A tropical storm.

The car stops moving on our way up a hill, and I peer out the left window and glimpse a stunning staircase leading up the cliff.

"Car won't go up, sir." The driver shifts. "We can wait out the rain . . . a couple of hours, at most . . ."

I can tell by Saint's flash of frustration that he's not spending an hour or two hiding from anything. Saint tips him. "We'll take the stairs."

He steps into the pouring rain. With one swift move, he scoops me out and into his arms. "Hang on," he says. He grins tenderly, and I laugh. Wet raindrops fringe his lashes. I grasp his wet neck and ball myself up from the rain, watching, enraptured, as a rivulet of rainwater slides down his throat and to his hard pecs. I want to catch it with my tongue, tongue him up, head to toe.

"We're going to get a cold!" I shout through the noise of the storm.

He presses his wet nose to my ear. "Maybe. I'll keep you warm."

"You're supposed to carry me through the door, not up a thousand steps."

"Well, there's the door."

I smile as we spot it, still dozens of steps away. The house sits atop a rocky cliff, looking at the sea and surrounded by green foliage swaying in the wind. Nothing but angry clouds above.

Malcolm gets us inside and sets me on my feet. We remove our shoes and leave my classic taupe pumps and his sleek black Guccis on the mat to dry. What is it about bare feet and men in jeans? My husband gets a thousand gold stars for hotness.

He surveys the house like a connoisseur as we both pad barefoot through its rooms. Him in jeans, me in my Vera Wang white skirt and jacket.

We'll be staying in this high-end Indonesian home, exotic and rustic on the outside, a city man's dream on the contemporary inside. Wide windows; wood ceiling beams, large and thick; smooth-looking contemporary furniture.

I set about to investigate while Saint welcomes the luggage the driver has lugged up the steps. I see that we have a fully stocked kitchen, macadamia butters and jellies stacked near the coffee and tea offerings.

Walking into the master bathroom, my damp feet squeaking with each step, I peer into the mirror . . . to the reality that I look like hell. My hair wet. My silk shirt caked to my body. My makeup streaked down my face. My Saint's perfect bride has just vanished—poof, back into the dream I imagined her from.

A heavy sense of inadequacy slaps me.

I scrub my face clean with soap and frantically try to brush my hair with my fingers. But I still don't look like the perfect, beautiful bride I wanted him to see.

FUCK. ME. RIGHT. *HERE.*

Urgh!!!!

A messy bride is so *not* what Saint deserves.

"That will be all," he says to the driver, then looks at me and closes the door.

Thunder crashes nearby. The wind whistles. There's a storm outside, billowing trees, fierce, but not as fierce as the storm inside. There's a storm inside my body, inside this room, and its name is Malcolm Saint. The storm within a storm, his force field protecting me, drawing me in with more power than any sweeping wind.

The tension that has been building all day thickens when he settles all the intensity of his attention on me.

A tingling awareness crawls over my skin. The kind I feel when he is near. I drink in every detail of his physique. The dark figure of him in the spectacularly large house, big and powerful. He stands there, devilishly handsome. Wet from head to toe. Those black jeans he wears so well hanging low on his hips, his muscular torso caked with rain. The scent of his soap reaches me. Suddenly I burn to make him breathless and groan, to feel his big body tighten for me. Quiver for me.

I want to lick his collarbone and feel and taste every inch of his gold velvet skin.

He starts coming forward, his eyes taking a leisurely trek across every inch of my body, as if he's savoring the sight of me too.

My voice feels thick as cotton when I shake my head and say, "I need . . . to fix myself."

"You're perfect."

"No, really, this isn't . . . you deserve for me to smell divine . . ." I trail off when Saint stops before me. Between those wet lashes of his, his eyes couldn't be more admiring or adoring of me.

"You smell like you—your shampoo, your soap, you, and rain."

"You smell like rain too."

He pulls the hair out of my face. "This is pretty perfect for me."

"You, looking at me like this. You're perfect." His wet clothes are sticking deliciously to his body. I reach out and squeeze his biceps. Hard as rock. I press up to him, closer. He tugs a button on my blouse open. Kisses there. Below my pulse point, on the little triangle of skin he revealed. He tugs another button open. Kisses there.

I reach out to do the same, freeing one button on his shirt.

He watches me through his lashes as I undo another.

"You want to go first?" He wipes my wet hair away as he asks, voice raspy like tree bark.

I nod.

I'm shivering.

"You cold? Want a bath?"

"No. I want you inside me." I push at his chest, urging him to lower himself to the nearest chair. I drop at his feet and work the rest of the buttons until I'm able to spread his shirt apart, revealing his muscled abs, his cut torso.

I run my fingers over his shoulders and push his shirt back, watching his chest flex as he shrugs it off.

My fingers wander over all the muscles and skin I just revealed. "Dibs on every part I kiss," I say.

He watches me, his eyes filling with a raw, deep longing as I lean forward to press kisses on his abs. Up his chest. He lets me, his muscles hardening under my fingers as I lean on him to brush my lips downward now as I unfasten his jeans.

I unzip him, and when he slowly comes to his feet, I'm readily pulling his jeans down his long, muscled, hair-dusted legs.

He's letting me, watching me, eye-fucking me.

When he's all golden, wet skin, he lowers himself again and I edge up to press my curves to his hard body. All these muscles are so perfectly natural, produced by sports. Polo. Skydiving. Yachting. The gym. Perfection.

"You missed a spot," he says huskily, sliding a hand up my back.

I kiss his hard-on as tenderly as I did the rest of him.

His expression is all wicked eyes and devil's grin. He trails his eyes over my face. "You tired?"

A pulsing knot within me demands more. "Not anymore."

He eases a tendril of wet hair behind my ear, and then he leans forward and whispers in my ear, "You are going to be really exhausted by the end of the night."

"Oh god, I'm so turned on right now."

He leads me up to my feet. "My turn."

I'm shaking wetly as he towers before me and looks possessively into my eyes. He unzips my damp white skirt. With a long, gentle tug, he eases it off my hips and it hits the floor. The scent of rain mingled with his shampoo invades the air as he opens up my shirt, his fingers slow and easy.

My knees go weak when I hear the long, hot breath he expels as he parts the fabric. Green eyes, violent with lust, admire my lacey, see-through panties and my matching bra. I can see by the way his pupils are dilating that Malcolm hasn't failed to notice the dusky pink of my nipples through the flimsy material.

His hands, expert and sure, continue easing off my shirt. He misses nothing as he strips my panties down my legs. He unhooks my bra, peeling it off my wet skin. His eyes sweep over me, approving and adoring. And then his hands stroke over my naked shape, drying me.

He ducks his head. His tongue flicks my earlobe, and then he turns my chin and he slides his lips over mine.

"Dibs on my wife," he rasps, and kisses my   mouth,

completely and thoroughly. I moan. His hands spread on my back, bringing me close to his naked body as he drops a fervent kiss on the back of my ear. "Dibs on this ear."

I laugh, so hot and bothered, my arms clench reflexively around his neck. Quakes overtake me as he runs his hands, flat and smooth, all over my curves, drying me some more.

He looks at me with this little smile when the sensations of his touch make me gasp, and his eyes are sparks of heat fixed on my face. They look so heavy, his eyes, his lashes dark, sweeping downward as he dips his head and drags his lips sinuously along my neck, to my collarbone, my shoulders, toward my very pulse point, now fluttering in the nook where the gold *R* and *M* necklaces lay nestled.

His tongue dips into the nook and he no doubt tastes the rain there. I shiver, uncontrollably, as the heat inside my body rises. My fingers trail up the wet muscles of his arms.

His lips seduce and sear my damp skin as they roam over my jaw, to my ear, and then head back to my mouth. My hands roam the grooves of his back, damp too. Then he takes my wrists and pulls my hands to my sides, walks me back, and rests them on the wall.

He interlaces our fingers, his grip strong as anchors, and starts to kiss my lips, softly. His body's still wet, but mine has been dried by his hands. I push upward to feel him, rubbing my breast against his flat chest, the wet making me ache.

"I need . . . god, I need you so much," I gasp in his ear.

He eases back. He loves foreplay, and he seems determined to make it last. He strokes the knuckles of one hand down my face. "Good so far?"

I'm suddenly overcome with butterflies inside.

I press my nose into his neck and close my eyes and let myself enjoy his fabulously manly smell. "Good. Get closer,

Malcolm, please."

My hands snake up the back of his neck, into his wet hair. His hands rub up my back. Before I know it, I tip my head back, he ducks his, and our lips are fusing together. I press myself to him, wanting him to devour me.

He lifts me to a table, his lids halfway down his eyes as he drinks me in.

Then my tongue is tracing his nipples; first one, in a neat wet circle, then the other. He reaches to brush the wet tendrils of my hair back and peers with intimate intensity into my face while my fingers trail down the ripples of his abs, toward the perfect V that dips into the mat of hair where his massive erection greets me.

"Did you miss me like I missed you, Rachel?" he whispers, cradling my breasts with his hands, thumbs tweaking. Sparks shoot off in me as I hold him in my hand.

I breathlessly nod. "So much."

I've had sex but it's crazy with him. I'm feverish. He's calm and collected, but he's so wired for me, his body hums and crackles with electricity.

He's hard and ready, the head of his lovely dick already wet, and I nibble his throat as I reach around his lean hips and grab part of his ass to get him closer.

When I rub his erection with the heel of my palm, he mock-chides, "All right, you're playing dirty now," lifts me up in his arms, walks us to the room, then lowers me on the plushest bed I've ever lain on.

He parts my legs with his hands, urging the inside of my thighs to fall open, and I grow even more restless when his green eyes settle on the part where I most ache.

"You," I plead. "Not your fingers or your tongue."

But my Saint is a Sinner, as we've already established.

He recklessly dives his head and explores me with his tongue a little, four deep, delicious strokes, then with his fingers, then he eases his hips between my parted legs. I throw my head back, a guttural sound in my throat. Our bodies light up, glowing like firestones.

When he slides the head inside, I rock wantonly and coax him to give me more.

He grabs my hip in one hand to hold me still.

"Oh god. You're perfect," I gasp.

He's thick and huge and pulsing, stretching me. When I'm full enough to burst, squirming and digging my nails into his back and kissing his shoulders, he sets the rhythm. Slow first. The glide of his cock in and out of me wreaks havoc with my body. I start shivering, rubbing his muscles, sucking his jaw, making throaty, unintelligible sounds.

I absorb the feel of him with my hands and body. His powerful legs, his abs and ass as he thrusts, his arms and chest and shoulders as he takes me. And me, soft and warm. Wet and hot. I'm eroticized by the way Saint is spreading me open and making me his wife.

"Malcolm, I'm so hot."

He groans and growls out, "Wet and hot and just how I like you."

Soon we're all instinct. Nails. Teeth. Sucking, kissing, biting, nibbling. He starts driving powerfully into me, fucking me into the bed while I suck fiendishly at his thick, juicy lower lip. He moves his lips, his tongue coming to spar with mine. A fever overtakes us, our bodies pressing and grinding. As we taste and tongue each other, the muscles of his back strain and ripple under my fingers.

He slows the pace, and my toes curl from the pleasure. My body arches and strains as he takes his cock fully out and rubs the head along my folds, over my clit. My eyes roll into the back of my head. When he slides back inside me, I purl in gratitude. "Malcolm." My eyes flutter open to see the tendons bulging on his neck, the harsh clamp of his jaw.

One animalistic groan from him, one from me—we come at the same time.

He's warm inside me, gripping me loosely against his body. He moves, whispering to me that he loves me. That he loves me so much.

Limp when we're done, I start to flush under his gaze. He's still inside me, and I cup his jaw and whisper in wonder, "Mr. Saint."

He drinks me up, green eyes looking at me reverently.

"Mrs. Saint." He rubs the corner of my lips with his thumb and when I press closer to the touch, his eyes grow even more tender. "God, I love you. I love you so much."

He brushes my hair back and looks into my face.

He strokes my mouth and frowns thoughtfully, an unmistakably playful light in his eyes. "Is it your mouth? You've got a spectacular set of lips, Mrs. Saint."

He's still frowning even as I smile up at him in delight.

"Your breasts are the perfect size, not too big, not too small, perky and so responsive. These eyes?"

His thumbs brush over my eyelids.

"Silver when you're angry, dark gray when you're melting in lust."

He strokes a hand down my leg next.

"Your long legs, that's got to be it. Or maybe . . ." His frown deepens as he touches my mouth's corners. "Your smiles and how genuine they are, the eagerness in your eyes as you watch life unfold around you."

I'm blushing and laughing, and he rolls to his back and

pulls me close, not frowning and not teasing now. But smiling. Smiling so beautifully at me.

"But see, it's the full package, and the fact that you make me whole. That void we've talked about before, it's gone when I've got you with me."

"Void." It's my turn to pretend to be puzzled. "What void? You fill my life to a bursting point."

Drawing me to him, he sets his head back on the pillow and lets out a long, easy laugh, and I crawl closer and lace my fingers at the back of his neck. "Hold me tight, Malcolm."

He presses a kiss to my forehead and tightens his hold on me and teasingly confesses, peering into my face, "All the time, I want to squeeze you to pieces, but then I wouldn't have you anymore. I can't have that." His face goes sober, deathly so, and even his voice grows dark. "I can't have that at all."

I forgot to tell my mother we'd arrived safely. She'd been nervous when we left, not knowing where we were going, and I promised to let her know the flight went all right.

I lift up my phone. No signal.

"Come here."

He inserts a chip into his computer.

"I brought technology with me. You get four minutes."

"Oh, come on. Five."

"Three now."

I laugh and open my account and shoot an email to my mother. This brief little glimpse of a computer makes me wonder about that world. If any wedding pictures are out there, of something that's just his and mine. I can imagine Tahoe telling the world. My friends telling their other friends. The media.

"Do you need to check anything?" I ask, glancing over my shoulder.

"Thirty seconds. Counting down."

He is making me pay, big-time and with *interest.*

I slap the laptop shut.

"Fine. I will settle my debt with you, husband."

I watch him watch me with a smirk as I crawl across the bed and slip into his now-too-familiar arms, the laptop and everything forgotten as I happily make it up to him, and I guess we are just too busy enjoying our Happily Ever After to give a shit.

It's the middle of the night, and our bodies aren't yet used to the time change. I've been tossing and turning for a few hours, while Malcolm stirs when I move and simply puts his hand on my waist—to still me or calm me or maybe to push my restless little body off the bed. He's pulled me closer though, and tighter.

He's almost crushing me now. Malcolm is spread out beside me, one arm folded under the pillow, his body facedown, neck twisted so his face is dipped into my neck.

I ease off with a breathless huff, then I kiss the disheveled dark hair before I walk naked to the window, trying to guess the time. A sliver of light steals through the green foliage out the window.

We're in the middle of nowhere. We're somewhere that doesn't exist anywhere else. Turns out Saint bought this house as a permanent getaway for us, with a brand-new bed, brand-new furniture, brand-new everything.

There's nothing within miles. The staff isn't supposed

to check in for days. Just him and me for the most perfect, hormone-indulging days.

If peace needed a dwelling in the world, this is where it would hide. If I could freeze a moment in time, I would choose the exact moment when he walks up behind me, wraps his arms around me, and kisses the back of my neck. When he says in the husky voice of a very-well-satisfied man, "Good morning, wife."

When I turn, bedroom green eyes look down at me as he snakes an arm around me and pulls me close . . . right into the spot. My favorite spot; the home base to baseball, the eye of any hurricane, the still center of the earth out from which everything spins. Right here. In two arms. Held by one man. My spot to come back after a spin. My spot to laugh, and love, and Sin.

ACKNOWLEDGMENTS

Extra-special thanks to everyone who's been following Malcolm and Rachel's journey together. I wasn't ready to let them go, and I hope you enjoy this novella where we got to spend some extra time with them and the cast!

Huge thanks to my author friends and betas who make the sometimes-long writing process a little bit less lonely; to   Kelli K. and Anita S.; to everyone at Gallery Books, including my editor, Adam Wilson; my publishers, Jen Bergstrom and Louise Burke; to all of my librarians, booksellers, Sullivan and Partners, every wonderful person at the Jane Rotrosen Agency—especially to the phenomenal Amy Tannenbaum—my foreign publishers, and my beautiful family, for your unconditional love and support.

And to all of the bloggers and readers who have been supporting me through the years, who give my book life in their minds and hearts, thank you for what you do and for letting me share my worlds and people with you.

Thank you!

ABOUT THE AUTHOR

Katy Evans is married and lives with her husband and their two children plus three lazy dogs in South Texas. Some of her favorite pastimes are hiking, reading, baking, and spending time with her friends and family. For more information on Katy Evans and her upcoming releases, check her out on the sites below. She loves to hear from her readers.

Website: www.katyevans.net
Facebook: https://www.facebook.com/AuthorKatyEvans
Twitter: https://twitter.com/authorkatyevans
Email: katyevansauthor@gmail.com

Books by Katy Evans

The Manwhore series

Manwhore

Manwhore +1

Ms. Manwhore

The REAL series

REAL

MINE

REMY

ROGUE

RIPPED

Copyright © 2015 by Katy Evans

ISBN 978-1517356422

CPSIA information can be obtained at www.ICGtesting.com
Printed in the USA
BVOW08s0334060916

461177BV00001B/4/P

9 781517 356422